# DEVIOUS

# DEVIOUS

BOOK FIVE IN THE ON THE RUN INTERNATIONAL
MYSTERIES

SARA ROSETT

DEVIOUS
Book Five in the *On the Run International Mysteries* series

Copyright © 2015 by Sara Rosett

Second Paperback Edition: March 2017
First Paperback Edition: 2015

ISBN: 978-0-9988431-0-0

# 1

THE CROWDS SHIFTED, AND ZOE lost sight of the man in the black shirt. She dodged to the left around a mom pushing a stroller and spotted the man again as he stepped onto one of the escalators in the mall. Zoe immediately reduced her pace and slipped into a store blasting pop music near the base of the escalator. She strolled along a table of sweaters near the front of the store, keeping an eye on the escalator through the large windows. She lingered beside a mannequin, but focused her attention out the window.

It was easy to keep him in sight as he rose up the escalator. She pushed down the urge to leave the store and made herself wait. He was hemmed in between two groups, and Zoe could only see a bit of his shirt and his wavy brown hair as the escalator traveled higher. As he neared the top, he turned, his gaze running over the people on the escalator below him, then his head swiveled as he widened his survey to include all of the marble-tiled area of the lower level. Zoe held her position, knowing that the mannequin shielded her. She squinted as she watched him and thought she saw a grin turn up the corners of his mouth. He whipped around, pushed his way through the group in front of him, then ran up the last few steps to the top of the escalator.

Zoe dropped the sweater and quickly strode out of the store. She hit the bottom step of the escalator and took the rest of the steps two at a time, muttering, "excuse me," as she raced around people standing still. Zoe throttled back on her speed as she neared the top and rode the last few feet up the escalator behind a rather ample woman, using the woman as a screen from the wide-open stretch of space at the exit of the escalator. Her heart hammering, not from the sprint up the stairs, but from the rush of the chase, Zoe scanned the upper level of the mall...but didn't see him anywhere.

She muttered under her breath as she stepped away from the escalator and moved to a kiosk selling coffee. He had to be here somewhere. He couldn't have gone far. She made a quick circuit of all the nearest stores, ducking in and out of a luggage store, a shoe store, and a Bath and Body Works. Those were the closest stores and none of them had dressing rooms...*where could he have gone?* It hadn't taken her that long to get up the escalator. She should have seen him, if he'd sprinted away or gone into one of the clothing stores that were positioned farther away from the escalator.

Her instinct was to take off, running to the farther stores, but she didn't do it. *When you're tailing someone, it's not always about speed.* Jack had said that to her last time when she'd lost the person she was following. Zoe turned in a quick circle. Just one more look. That's when she saw it. A narrow corridor that branched off the main area with a tiny sign above it that read, RESTROOMS.

Now it was Zoe's turn to smile. She took a seat in a group of chairs near the coffee kiosk, turned toward the hallway. Her heart rate had returned to normal by the time the man emerged from the restroom.

He looked directly at her, a wide smile splitting his face. "Well done." He dropped into a chair beside her.

"Thanks, Jack." Zoe couldn't quite keep the smugness out of her tone. "Clever, going in the restroom."

"Yes, but you caught it. I didn't see you at all on the escalator."

"See, I have been paying attention. You're a good teacher."

Jack's silvery blue eyes twinkled, which punctured Zoe's exhilaration. "Why are you looking at me like that?"

"Like what?"

"Like you won this round. You didn't. I tailed you the whole way, and when you tried to give me the slip, I caught you."

"Yes, but you've got one more thing to learn."

"Not more car surveillance. We did that all last week. I don't want to spend another hour in the car."

"Just be glad it's January, not July."

"Yes, that would have been worse," she said, thinking of sweltering summers in Dallas. "Although, if I'd known exactly how boring your work could be, I might not have been so anxious to learn the ropes."

Up until a few months ago, Zoe had juggled several part-time jobs, ranging from freelance copy editor to dog walker to virtual assistant, but recently she'd decided to shift away from those jobs after she and Jack had an interesting encounter during a trip to Rome last year. They had met Harrington Throckmorton, an insurance man with the reputable and well-known Millbank and Proust Company. Harrington was planning to take early retirement then open his own insurance investigation firm. He had asked both Zoe and Jack to work for him as consultants. Zoe had jumped at the chance. Hopscotching from one temp job to the next had begun to lose its allure, and working with Harrington sounded interesting. Jack, who already had his own security consulting firm up and running, said working with Harrington would only increase their standing with clients.

Zoe and Jack had returned from Rome, and Zoe had expected a call from Harrington daily, but cutting ties with Millbank and Proust had taken longer than Harrington had anticipated. He got wrapped up in a complex case that took quite a while to finish, but two months ago he'd officially retired and began contacting Zoe with small commissions, mostly things that could be handled via computer.

Zoe figured that while she was waiting for a bigger assignment from Harrington it would be a good time to learn some of Jack's special skills. He had what he termed a "varied" past, which included more than security work, and sometimes his consulting firm took on projects that were more than installing security systems or checking for weak points in existing systems. One of those special skills had been how to tail someone without being spotted. It wasn't a skill she thought she needed, but life had taken some surprising turns recently, and there was more than one time that knowing how to do it would have come in handy. Jack had shown her how to tail someone both on foot and in a car, then he'd brought her along on one of his surveillance gigs.

"Oh, come on," Jack said. "Sitting on a warehouse for three days couldn't be any more boring than all those spreadsheets you used to do."

"True," Zoe admitted reluctantly. "But I was able to take a bathroom break whenever I wanted, something that I never truly appreciated."

"Every job has its downsides. And monitoring that location will bring in a good chunk of cash."

"Yes, the ability not to be overdrawn at the bank is a good thing." For most of her life, Zoe's bank balance had skated dangerously close to dipping into the red. "I hate to say this, but I'm beginning to understand why Helen was constantly nagging at me to get a steadier job. Having some cushion in our bank account is a strange and comforting feeling." They had even been able to sock away some money in a savings account, a *joint* savings account. Her best friend, Helen, had never understood Zoe's desire not to be tied down to one job. "But I shouldn't call it nagging. I'm sure Helen thought of it as watching out for me."

"How is Helen feeling?"

"Puking her guts out. The first trimester is rough. Her doc says if she can get through another four weeks, she'll probably feel better." Zoe checked her phone. "In fact, I should go. I'm taking her some soup today."

"Before you go, there's one more lesson for today."

Zoe pulled her keys out of her pocket. "What? Don't hit the bathroom when you're on the run?"

"No. Always check behind you." Jack looked over Zoe's shoulder and nodded. "When you're tailing someone, don't be so focused on the person you're following that you forget to check behind you for someone tailing *you*."

Zoe swiveled around and groaned. Her friend Carla sat on a bench a couple of feet away, sipping from a coffee cup. She raised her cup, a salute, and grinned then came over to Zoe and Jack, her cowboy boots slapping on the marble floor. She plopped down on the chair on the other side of Zoe with a *thunk* that made her blond ponytail bounce. "That was fun." She wrinkled her upturned nose at Zoe. "You didn't even see me, did you?"

"No. At the very least, I should have heard the thud of those boots. Were you behind me all the time?"

"Every second. Most fun I've had since I found the backdoor into the First Bank and Trust system."

With her swingy mohair sweater and skinny jeans, you'd never suspect Carla was one of the top computer security experts in the southwest.

A few bars of *Smoke on the Water* filled the air, and Carla pulled her phone out of her back pocket. "I have to go. More websites to hack, but let me know if you need me again, Jack."

"I don't think I will. Zoe is a quick study."

"Yeah. I won't make that mistake again," Zoe said as Carla pounded away.

Jack stood. "Hey, you're a kinesthetic learner—hands on. You'll remember that now, better than if I just told you."

"Right. I'll be so jumpy and skittish I'll spend the whole time I'm tailing someone looking over my shoulder now. I'll probably be so focused on what's going on behind me that I'll forget to keep an eye on the actual person."

"I doubt that. Want a coffee?"

"Sure."

While they were waiting for their coffee, Zoe's phone chimed. "It's Harrington," she said to Jack before answering. She put the phone to her ear. "Harrington, good to hear from you."

"It is always lovely to hear your voice as well, Zoe," Harrington said, and Zoe couldn't help but smile. His perfect manners matched his polished British accent. "Do you have a few moments?"

"Yes, of course." Jack handed Zoe her coffee, and they moved to the escalator.

"Excellent," Harrington said. "I have a job for you, if you're interested. The daughter of a family friend has contacted me with a request to recover a stolen painting. I'd handle it myself, but I'm currently involved in a rather delicate manner that involves Interpol and the Guardia Civil, and I can't get away. I have a contact in the area where the painting was stolen. She should be able to help you run it down. Would you be interested?"

"Yes, of course. Where did the painting go missing from?"

"Staircase House in Edinburgh. Would you be able to leave fairly soon? Time is of the essence with these things."

"How about tomorrow?"

"Excellent. I'll have my assistant make the travel arrangements. I'm afraid I have a meeting in a few moments that I must attend. I can call you back in a few hours with all the details."

"Sounds great. I'll go pack and wait for your call back."

Zoe ended the call and turned to Jack. "I'm going to Edinburgh."

2

---

ZOE TOSSED A RAINCOAT INTO her suitcase, then pulled it out again. "No, this should go on top, where I can get to it," she murmured to herself, moving it to another pile on the bed.

Jack came out of the bathroom, carrying his shaving kit. "So Harrington called you back with the details?"

"Yes, just got off the phone with him a few minutes ago." Zoe reached for her notepad. "The client is Poppy Foley, oldest daughter of the extremely wealthy Foley family. Harrington knew the father, Lorne, who recently passed away—just a few weeks ago. Harrington sounded pretty upset. He said they went to school together. A Victorian painting has gone missing after a break-in at their Edinburgh home, which tells you how well-off they are. They have a flat in London, the house in Edinburgh, and a country estate in Devon."

"What's the painting?"

"A small landscape painted by one of their ancestors." Zoe

consulted the paper. "Annabel Foley. It's not a masterpiece or anything. It only has a sentimental value to the family. Poppy hired Harrington because she wants to make sure the painting is recovered, but she wants to keep the theft of it quiet. Her mother is still dealing with her father's death, and Poppy wants to take care of this. Her mother has always been attached to the painting and would apparently take its loss hard."

"Anything else missing?"

"Not according to Harrington, but he didn't have much time. He's sending me an email with all his notes."

Zoe moved to the dresser. "This is going to work out perfectly. We can drive to the airport together tomorrow, and each take our separate flights."

"Right." Jack smoothed the folds of the umbrella down and swirled it in his hand, compressing the folds.

Something in his voice made Zoe look up from her drawer. "You're okay with this, aren't you?"

"Yeah, sure." Jack fastened the little strip of Velcro that kept the umbrella furled.

Zoe crossed her arms, pressing a stack of long-sleeved T-shirts against her chest. "You don't sound okay."

Jack tossed the umbrella into one of the open suitcases, which rested on the bed between them. He ran his fingers through his hair. "No. It's fine. You'll go to Edinburgh. Harrington will put you in touch with his art dealer contact, and I'm sure you'll get it taken care of. You'll probably have the painting back in a few days."

Zoe put the shirts in the suitcase then folded one leg under herself, sat down on the bed, and reached for a pile of socks. "I get it. You wish you were going."

Jack had stepped into the closet and for a moment there was only the clatter of hangers then he stepped out, holding several dress shirts. "Of course, I wish I was going with you." He dropped the shirts by his suitcase. "I just assumed that the first official case for Harrington would be a joint thing."

"Well, I'm sure he wouldn't mind you going, especially if we paid for your airfare, but you have the conference in Houston. You can't cancel." Jack had been scheduled to give a presentation on physical and cyber security at a conference for small business owners for over a year.

"No, I can't." Jack's face was tight. "I want to, but I can't."

Zoe dropped the socks she'd been matching. "Do you think I can't do this?"

"No, of course not." Jack left the shirts and came to sit beside her. "We work best together, that's all. I've seen it these last few months."

Zoe studied his face for a moment. "There's a smidgen of worry there. I can see it."

"I'd be worried about you, if you were staying here. I always worry about you."

Zoe smiled and kissed him quickly. "I know. It's a sweet quality you have, that you worry about me."

"And you don't worry enough."

"No, you worry too much. I worry just the right amount. Do you want me to call Harrington back and tell him I can't take the job?"

"No."

"Good. Because I wouldn't want to do that."

"You'd do the job anyway, even if I didn't want you to do it?" Jack said, a small smile on his face. "I know there's no stopping you once you get going."

"I could ask Harrington if I could delay a day or two, but time is of the essence. We'll just have to be good together long-distance. We do have these things called phones, you know. Amazing tech. Lets you talk to someone as if they were in the room with you."

Jack closed the distance between them. "But you can't do this over the phone," he said, dropping a few light kisses on her mouth.

"Then we better do as much of this while we can."

<hr/>

Zoe tightened her seatbelt as the airplane began its descent. For most of the journey, there had only been inky blackness out the window, but now pinpricks of light, miles and miles of light, spread out below the plane, running up to the edge of the estuary with, in Zoe's opinion, the best ever name for a body of water, the Firth of Forth. She'd spent the early part of the flight scanning the guidebook she'd brought along, going over the landmarks and layout of the city.

She glanced at the empty seat beside her. The confidence she had felt about handling the recovery of the painting on her own had faded. She and Jack had been inseparable for months, working in tandem, mostly on his projects, but they'd also taken to doing mundane tasks like cleaning the house and keeping up the yard together. It felt odd not to have him beside her for this new challenge, her first real case for Throckmorton Enquiries, Incorporated. She wanted to do a good job —do Harrington proud, but as she looked at those millions of lights, the enormity of the task settled on her. How could she find a single tiny painting among that huge city? And there was no guarantee the painting was still in Edinburgh either. What if it had been moved out of the city? The trail was several days old.

The pilot came on, announcing their descent, and a flurry of movement filled the cabin as people closed tray tables and shuffled their belongings under seats. Zoe gave herself a mental shake. Sure, it would be great if Jack could be here, but he couldn't be, so she'd just have to do it on her own—as she had for so many years before she met Jack. She'd run down a few missing things, not to mention people, by herself. She'd give it her level best shot to make it happen again.

She turned her attention back to the window and enjoyed watching the tiny cars and minuscule roads grow larger. She'd always wanted to travel, and these last few months had brought several trips, which had allowed her to see some amazing sights. One of her steadier freelance gigs had been copy-editing travel guide books for *Smart Travel*, and she'd always enjoyed reading about the tourist sites, traveling vicariously through her work, but now here she was in a new place. She'd never been to Scotland, and couldn't wait to see it for herself. It didn't matter how much you'd read about a place, the only way to truly know it was to experience it yourself.

After negotiating customs, Zoe emerged from the airport

onto the slick wet pavement and signaled for a cab. It wasn't raining at the moment, but the air felt thick and heavy with moisture. One of the neat black cabs similar to the ones she'd seen in London stopped beside her, and she gave the address of her hotel. Harrington hadn't splurged for a business class ticket, but he had arranged for an extremely early check-in at the hotel. She gave the address and settled back to watch the city. Around the airport and for most of the drive, Edinburgh was a modern city, but a sign for the city center loomed, and then the cab moved into an area of cobblestoned streets and aged stone buildings.

Her hotel was in the heart of Edinburgh. Tall stone pillars framed the glass entrance doors, but inside, bright colors and curvy modern furniture dominated the lobby. The elevator was painted like one of Kate Spade's bold rainbow striped handbags, and the walls in her room were painted in turquoise and violet. The bright colors and contemporary furniture seemed an odd mix with the old and historic buildings out the window. The first rays of sunrise were illuminating the rooftops. A padded envelope with her name in Harrington's precise printing had been waiting for her at the front desk. Now that she was in her room, Zoe ripped it open.

"Wow." A thick stack of twenty-pound notes filled the envelope. Zoe pulled out the single thick sheet of cream paper. *For purchase of the painting, if needed. H.*

Sending cash made sense. If she located the painting, she might have to buy it back. They weren't the police. Their focus wasn't to catch the thief, only to find and return the painting. She and Harrington had discussed the moral ins-and-outs of their position at the dinner when he'd asked both her and Jack to work with him.

"The culprit is not our objective," he'd said. "It is a nice dividend. Ideally, the successful conclusion of a case would involve both the recovery of the missing item and the capture of the guilty party."

Such a large wad of cash made her a bit nervous. After she closed the envelope and stashed it in the room safe, she felt better. She whipped the curtains closed, took a shower, and set an alarm on her new phone for noon. Her appointments to meet with the client and with Harrington's contact weren't until that afternoon, so she could get a few hours of rest. She set her new phone down on the nightstand and crawled under the covers. When the security consulting business began to make a little money, the first thing Jack had done was buy Zoe a smartphone to replace her rather ancient flip phone. She had argued that she didn't need it, but Jack had insisted that it was a business expense and that she needed it. After a few months of use, Zoe had to admit that it had plenty of handy features like the alarm, and having the Internet at her fingertips was a bonus. She dropped into bed and didn't have a bit of trouble falling asleep.

By twelve-thirty, Zoe was bundled in her raincoat and had her umbrella tucked under her arm along with the directions to both the client's house and Harrington's contact. She walked toward the Royal Mile, the cobblestone road that cut through the center of historic Edinburgh. A few hours of deep sleep, coupled with a strong cup of coffee from the coffeemaker in her room had her feeling rejuvenated and ready to tackle the day. Even though it felt like morning to Zoe, the days were short this time of year, and the sun was already past its zenith and sliding toward the horizon. Her hotel was only a few blocks from the Royal Mile, Edinburgh's oldest street. She knew she'd arrived when she saw the swinging pub sign for Deacon Brodie's Tavern, which depicted the dual personalities of the man who had inspired Robert Louis Stevenson's tale of *Dr. Jekyll and Mr. Hyde.* One side of the sign showed a respectable colonial gentleman holding keys, which Zoe remembered from her guidebook reading, represented his job as a cabinet and lock installer. Zoe walked under the sign and looked up. The opposite side depicted him masked and holding a bag of loot. Using the keys he had access to through his work, Brodie became a thief, even organizing other criminals into gangs until he was caught and executed. Zoe read the gold plaque that described how he'd been hung on Edinburgh's gallows.

The cold wind tugged at Zoe's hair, swishing some strands of it around her face. She tucked her hair behind her ears and turned away from the tavern with a shiver that was only partly due to the frigid air. She stopped for a quick sandwich at a pub, then followed the directions Harrington had sent her and moved up the street toward Edinburgh Castle, which loomed a head in the distance. Between the gothic arches, mullioned windows, and the many souvenir shops selling kilts, cashmere, and kitschy miniature replicas of the castle, small alcoves led from the main street to interior courtyards, or "closes" beyond the main street. Zoe found the one with a sign for John's Close and followed the pointing arrow through the arched tunnel and emerged into a paved courtyard area with a single central light post. Houses three, four, and five-stories tall enclosed the sloping courtyard. Some of the houses were made of stucco and painted a mellow cream or gray, while others were built of brown and yellow stone.

Harrington had said, "Staircase House is the one with the turret. You can't miss it." The curved tower that dominated one of the smaller buildings did standout. Zoe checked the time. She was early, but she was here, so she crossed to the house. The curved turret, which was situated on one corner of the building, ran all the way from the ground floor and extended above the main roofline of the building. The turret was topped with a little spire on its roof. A door was set into the curved wall. Zoe found a bell and pressed. She waited, nodding to a few people who passed through the close. She rang the bell again and waited a few more minutes. There were a couple of windows set into the building low to the ground, in what must be a basement area, but they were barred and the interior was dark, so Zoe turned away. She'd have to return at the appointment time, in roughly an hour.

She emerged back onto the Royal Mile. The castle tempted her, but she knew better than to visit a historic monument with only an hour to tour it. She walked a few more blocks and turned onto another cobblestoned street lined with tall buildings. Shops and restaurants lined the street level on both sides of the curving street, their storefronts painted cheerful red, blue, and yellow. A balcony-like walkway ran along the top of the shops, creating another level of stores set back above the road.

Harrington's contact owned a shop on the main road, the Blue Door, a gallery with the trim around the windows and door painted royal blue. Several paintings along with a set of candlesticks, an ancient top hat, five antique globes, and a violin were displayed in the windows. Zoe pushed open the door, setting of a chime of bells. The shop smelled strongly of vanilla candles with a few low notes of musty, dusty things. A woman in her fifties came forward, her dark blond pageboy swinging with every step. She wore a navy turtleneck, which accented her pale blue eyes, along with a long skirt and high-heeled boots. "Looking for anything particular today?"

"Yes, Violet Buchanan. Is she here?"

She raised carefully plucked eyebrows. "That's me. How can I help you?"

"I'm Zoe Andrews," Zoe said, glad her "new" married name rolled off her tongue so easily now. It had only taken a year or so to get used to it. "Harrington Throckmorton told me to get in touch with you. Have you heard from him?"

"Oh, yes." Her expression, which had been the shopkeeper's polite veneer changed and softened at the mention of Harrington's name. "He said you'd stop by. I didn't expect you until later." Violet's voice had a trace of a brogue to it, but unlike Zoe's interaction with the taxi driver—Zoe had smiled and nodded at what she hoped were appropriate times—she could understand Violet easily.

"I had time, so I figured I'd stop in now, if that's okay."

"Yes, fine. Come this way, please. We're not busy right now. We shouldn't be disturbed." She motioned for Zoe to follow her through the narrow shop. She pushed open a pair of swinging louvered half-doors, holding one open for Zoe after she passed through. The doors closed off a small office area from the main part of the shop. Violet indicated a wicker chair tucked into a crevice between a wooden desk and the wall, and Zoe slid into the chair. Violet offered Zoe something to drink, but Zoe said, "Thank you. I'm fine."

Violet took a seat in an antique rolling wooden desk chair and removed a folder from a vertical stacked file in front of her. The stacked files and a calendar blotter were the only items on the desk. Zoe studied the expanse of polished wood in awe. Jack had moved his office downstairs to one corner of the kitchen, but Zoe continued to use the kitchen island as her desk, which was usually covered in a scatter of papers and her laptop, as well as miscellaneous bills and junk mail.

Violet used one finger to flip the file open. It contained a photograph of the stolen painting, the same photograph that Harrington had sent to Zoe. She picked it up. "*A View of Edinburgh.*"

"Do you recognize the painting?" Zoe asked.

"Not this painting specifically, but I am familiar with the artist, Annabel Foley. I hate to make unequivocal statements without seeing the actual painting, but I believe she painted this quite early in her career. Have you heard of her?"

"No."

Violet swiveled and pulled a book down from a shelf. "She was born in 1830 in London. Her family was quite wealthy, and she traveled extensively through the British Isles during her early years. She never married. She painted her whole life, beginning with mostly landscapes. She went on to focus on flowers, painting them in nature as she discovered them. They're exquisite." She handed the book to Zoe, open to images of botanical paintings on facing pages. Both paintings were of a magnolia blossom, but one painting showed the flower as a bud, while the other showed it open in full bloom. The paintings were incredibly detailed. Each petal, leaf, and even the veins in the leaves were meticulously recorded. But the paintings weren't simply anatomically exact, there was something more that the artist had managed to capture. "They're so...vibrant."

"Yes, exactly. Foley is famous for the energy of her canvas. For instance, these magnolias seem to sway in the breeze."

"And it's interesting to see the flower at different stages," Zoe said, her gaze skipping back and forth as she looked at the similarities and differences.

"Annabel frequently painted a series of the same object at different growth stages or in different seasons. It was her trademark."

"Like Monet's paintings of the haystacks or the cathedral."

Violet nodded. "Exactly. Quite forward thinking for her day. She was the same way with the materials she used. She painted in oil at a time when ladies were supposed to paint in watercolor. Thank goodness she used oil. Watercolor doesn't endure as well as oil."

Violet turned back to the photograph of the landscape. She tapped the edge. "I didn't even know this painting existed. Female Victorian artists have been sadly overlooked in the past. It's only recently that they've been appreciated as much as their male colleagues. There's not even a complete catalogue of Foley's work." She paused and gave a rueful smile. "Bit of a hobbyhorse of mine, under-appreciated women painters from any era, but especially from Victorian times." She pointed to the photograph. "It's Edinburgh, of course, painted from the top of Arthur's Seat, I'm guessing. Do you know it?"

"Yes, I've heard of it. Haven't been to the top, but I've read about it." Zoe had read up on the park near Holyrood Palace. Its highest point was a dormant volcano called Arthur's Seat.

"The unique flora there would have interested her greatly, I imagine," Violet murmured. She took out a magnifying glass and leaned close over the photograph. "She would have painted it sometime after 1844 as the Scott Monument is complete," she said, touching the gothic monument that towered over the city skyline. I might be able to narrow it down to a more exact date by examining the various buildings, but that would take some time."

"I don't think you need to do that, at least not at this point," Zoe said. Violet was taking a purely academic interest in the painting. Zoe was more worried about the whereabouts of the painting, not where it fit in Foley's catalogue of artwork. "Harrington said you would have some possible leads on the location of the painting."

"Yes, that's the interesting part." Violet propped her elbows on the desk and leaned forward. "I checked with the police, and they've had no report of it being stolen."

"The family wanted to keep it quiet," Zoe said quickly.

Violet immediately straightened. "Oh, don't worry. I didn't tell the police it was missing. I have a contact. He works in a civilian capacity at the police force and can check these things for me. Very discreetly, you understand."

*I hope so,* Zoe thought. "So no leads with the police? Anything else?" Zoe asked a bit doubtfully. Violet didn't look like the type of person with connections on the seedy side of Edinburgh. If it had to do with a cocktail party or a gallery opening, Zoe bet Violet would be all over it, but shady art dealings? Zoe didn't think that was Violet's scene.

"I've contacted two people who are in that..." she waved her hand in a little circle, "area of the art trade. I don't toy with things of this nature myself." She touched the photograph. "But the art world is small. If someone has this or knows about it being taken, I'll hear something."

"How soon do you think that might be?"

"By tomorrow, at the latest. I made it clear that I needed to know as soon as possible. Now," she pulled a cell phone from a drawer. "Let me have your mobile phone number. I'll call you the moment I hear something."

Zoe exited the shop a few minutes later and called Jack as she walked back up the steep street to the Royal Mile. It was early in Houston, but she knew he'd be awake. Jack was not someone who lounged around sleeping in. He answered on the first ring. "Hey. How are you?"

"Making the rounds. Do you have a few minutes? I can't remember your schedule." A light mist filled the air, but it wasn't heavy enough for Zoe to bother with the umbrella. She was glad she'd pulled her long hair into a ponytail before she left the hotel. Humidity made her naturally curly hair coil even tighter than normal, but with it off her face, it could frizz away. She'd figured Scotland was not the place to flat iron her hair.

"Sure," Jack said. "I just finished setting up for my presentation. It doesn't start for thirty minutes."

"Okay, good. I met with Harrington's contact. I don't think she's going to be much help."

"Really? It wouldn't be like Harrington to send you to someone who doesn't know their stuff." Snatches of conversation and other ambient noise came over the line, making it hard to hear Jack.

Zoe pressed the phone harder to her ear. "Oh, she knows her stuff all right. She knows Victorian paintings and could tell me all about the artist and her career. She says she's put the word out about the painting, but I don't think I should count on hearing anything from her. She's an elegant woman. Cocktail parties and fundraisers for art causes seem more her line. I was thinking of calling Masard."

Henri Masard was an art dealer Zoe and Jack met in Paris who had helped them out of a scrape. He had a *laissez-faire* attitude toward the art that came through his shop, contacting the police now and again. Zoe thought he probably walked a fine line, staying mostly on the legal side of things and straying into more murky territory occasionally.

After a beat of silence, Jack said, "He might be helpful. You'll have to tell Harrington the whole situation, float the idea of contacting Masard, and see where he wants you to go from there."

"I know." Zoe blew out a sigh.

The ambient noise faded and Jack's voice came in stronger, his tone concerned. "What's wrong?"

"Harrington didn't send me here to follow a checklist and then report back to him and await my next instructions. He sent me here to get the painting back. He likes the innovative way I do things. He's told me that. It's one of the reasons he offered me this consulting job. I need to...I don't know...come up with some way of tracking the painting on my own."

"Zoe, we're partners with Harrington. Keep him updated... while you innovate. He won't appreciate being kept in the dark. If one of his contacts can't help you, he needs to know."

"I suppose that's true. I just don't want it to look like I don't know what to do without him telling me." Zoe reached the Royal Mile and paused at a crosswalk, waiting for a light. "Although, that's how I feel." The light changed, and she walked across the street. "Maybe the daughter will have some news for me. I'm on my way to meet her now. I'll have to call Harrington later."

"I see your feint there—that change of subject."

"Sometimes I think you know me too well." Zoe couldn't help the smile that crept onto her face.

"I've got a line on a couple of your moves, that's all. Good luck with the daughter. Let me know how it goes."

"I will. And good luck to you, on the presentation."

Jack made a grumbling sound. He wasn't exactly fond of speaking in front of a crowd. He'd spent most of his life avoiding attention. Being in the spotlight made Zoe's normally cool and collected husband sweat bullets, but they'd worked hard on prepping him for his presentation.

"You're going to do fine. This is where all those video recordings pay off."

"Yeah. I want evidence that you deleted those, by the way."

"Of course." Zoe moved through the arched tunnel entry to John's Close.

"Zoe," Jack said in a warning tone.

"See," Zoe said, exasperated. "You do know me too well. Some of those bloopers were just too funny to delete, but fine. I'll delete them."

"Zoe."

"I will as soon as I get home. I promise."

"Thank you."

"Don't think about that now," Zoe said. "You'll do great. You know your stuff, and I know you look terrific." Jack would wear one of his Italian suits that he'd picked up on sale during his time working at the consulate in Naples.

"You'll be fine, too. You'll figure out something. Just stay safe."

"I will. Oh, I think that's the daughter. I have to go." As Zoe crossed the courtyard, a woman with short brown hair wearing a dark trench coat and carrying a bag of groceries with a loaf of bread sticking out of it walked to the door set in the turret of Staircase House.

## 3

Z OE PICKED UP HER PACE and joined the woman at the door. "Hello. Are you Poppy Foley?"

The woman jerked toward Zoe with a sharp intake of breath.

"Sorry, I didn't mean to startle you. I'm Zoe Andrews. I work with Harrington Throckmorton. I'm here about the painting."

"Oh right." She put out her hand. "Nice to meet you. Let me get this unlocked, and we can get inside." Poppy was shorter than Zoe, about five feet tall, and had slightly protruding brown eyes and a long, narrow nose. The mist layered a fine spray of water over both of them. Poppy didn't have an umbrella either, and she had the same type of hair as Zoe's. Her chin-length bob was curling into spiral strands under the moisture. Poppy found the key she wanted and opened a thoroughly modern deadbolt that looked a bit at odds with the aged, rough wood of the door that was studded with iron.

The wood of the door around the lock and along the frame had the same antique look, but no fresh scars or gouges marred the wood. Zoe had learned a few things from Jack about security. "So either the intruder didn't get in this way, or they had a key," Zoe said as she followed Poppy onto the small landing of a circular staircase, which curved up to higher floors and down to the basement.

"What?" Poppy turned in the small area and looked back at the open door.

"The break-in. When the painting was stolen. This door wasn't damaged."

"No. It wasn't." Poppy reached around Zoe and closed the door. "The window upstairs was broken. That's how they got in. Do you mind setting the bolt? Thanks."

Zoe locked the door then followed Poppy up the steps toward the first floor.

Poppy continued speaking over her shoulder. "We get so many tourists, mostly architecture buffs, asking if they can take a quick look around." She rolled her eyes. "And then they pester you with questions about building materials and dates of construction, which I don't know anything about. The only thing I do know is that this house was built in 1622 and has many original features."

Zoe followed Poppy up the curving stone staircase. The lower half of the walls enclosing the staircase were painted a rich red while the upper half was cream. At the next floor, the second story, Poppy stepped onto another small landing and moved through a doorway into a long airy room painted in the same deep red tone as the staircase. Oak trim lined the walls as well as the tall windows that reached all the way to the high ceiling. A fireplace dominated the right side of the room while an oak bannister enclosing a minstrel's gallery ran along the upper portion of the left side of the room. Despite the dark wood trim and dark walls, the high ceiling and floor-to-ceiling windows gave the room an open feeling.

Poppy set down the groceries on a table near the door and dropped her purse beside it. "Can I take your coat?" She shrugged out of her own trench coat.

"Yes, thank you," Zoe handed off her raincoat, which Poppy hung on a coat tree by the door. After Zoe removed a small spiral notebook, pen, and her phone from her messenger bag, she placed her bag on the table by Poppy's purse. Since she'd never done this before, she wasn't quite sure what she'd need, but a pen and paper seemed a good thing to have.

"All right. Where would you like to start?" Poppy straightened the hem of her pink cardigan, then fidgeted with her hands, finally shoving them in the pockets of her black pants. A burglary tends to make people jittery, so Zoe didn't start with that topic. Instead she said, "First let me tell you that Harrington is so sorry he couldn't be here in person."

Poppy smiled. "Dear Uncle Harry. He's not really my uncle, of course. We just called him that when we were kids, my brother and I. He came to visit us quite a bit at Frampton Downs."

Harrington hadn't mentioned the name of the Foley's country estate, but Zoe assumed that was what Poppy was referring to.

Poppy looked more at ease as she continued, "I wish Uncle Harry could have been here, too, but I have complete confidence in you. He wouldn't send someone who couldn't complete the job."

Zoe's insides twisted, thinking that with only chic Violet in her corner, the odds of finding the painting were long, but Zoe put on her most reassuring and confident smile. "Thank you. Now, why don't you show me where the painting was located?"

"Yes, of course. That's the logical place to start. This way." She headed for another staircase located under the minstrel's gallery. The staircase ran straight up the wall to the gallery. "Mind this step." She pointed to a step about halfway up the staircase that was painted white, a contrasting color to the rest of the cream colored steps. "It was intentionally made higher than the others so that an intruder would stumble on it and give themselves away."

"Very clever. An early burglar alarm," Zoe said, filing the tidbit away to tell Jack. He'd find it interesting.

"Yes, unfortunately it didn't do a thing to prevent someone from taking Aunt Annabel's *View of Edinburgh*." Poppy walked along the narrow passage at the top of the stairs. It opened out into the minstrel's gallery, a loft-type area that overlooked the room below. A couple of chairs covered in a faded floral print fabric and a small desk filled the space. The walls, edged in dark wood trim, were covered in groupings of artwork, which included paintings and some photographs that looked as if they'd been taken shortly after the invention of the camera.

Poppy stopped in front of what had been a grouping of three paintings. "It was here." She pointed to the empty space between two gorgeous oil paintings of date palms done in vibrant colors, obviously some of Annabel Foley's later work.

"These are gorgeous," Zoe said, studying the remaining paintings.

"Yes, they're lovely." Poppy shook her head. "I don't understand why they didn't take these as well. I mean, I'm so glad they didn't, but it is rather odd."

"Yes, strange," Zoe murmured. Harrington had included the dimensions of the painting, nine inches by seven inches, slightly bigger than a sheet of typing paper. "Do you mind if I take some photos?" Zoe asked, thinking that it would be so easy to slip the painting into a backpack or even a large handbag.

"Go ahead." Poppy stepped back, her hands buried in her pockets.

Zoe used the camera on her phone to photograph the space where the painting had been then took close-ups of the paintings on each side of the blank spot.

"Why are you interested in these other paintings?" Poppy asked.

Zoe couldn't say, *I'm winging it here*, so she replied, "Just being thorough."

"Oh. Well, I'll leave you to it..." Poppy trailed off uncertainly as she backed toward the staircase.

"Wait. Can you show me where the break-in happened?"

"That window there." Poppy pointed beyond Zoe's shoulder to a large window near the seating area of the loft. "It was broken, but it's been repaired."

Zoe moved to the window and photographed it. Most of the panes of glass were wavy with age, giving the impression that you were looking through thick, syrupy air that had somehow broken the laws of nature and been frozen in place. Two panes near the lever-like handle that opened the window were filled with glass so clear that Zoe could see a few dust motes floating outside the window. A fire escape hugged the building outside the window ledge. "Do you mind if I open it?"

"No, go ahead."

"There's no alarm?" Zoe asked.

Poppy laughed briefly. "Well, yes, there is an alarm system, but it was installed in the early eighties. I don't think it's been used for ten years. It's so glitchy, we don't even bother to set it."

After a brief struggle with the latch, Zoe pushed the window open, letting in a cold draft. She leaned out and quickly photographed the metal fire escape as well as the window ledge. Zoe was pretty sure they didn't have metal fire escapes when the building was constructed in 1622, but it didn't look much newer than that. She wasn't going out on it. She quickly closed and refastened the window then turned back to Poppy, who was gathering up several papers that had blown off a nearby desk in the sudden gust of wind.

She handed them to Zoe. "This is all the information I have about the painting."

"Thanks." Zoe flicked through the thin stack. She didn't see anything that she hadn't already read in Harrington's briefing. In fact, Violet had told her more about the painting itself than the sketchy information in these papers. The last item in the file was a large photograph of the painting. Zoe pulled it out and examined it. It was larger than the image Harrington had attached to his email.

Poppy said, "It's a little blurry. It was a group photo taken up here. I cropped the people out and blew it up as large as I could. Uncle Harry said to give you any photos of the painting. This is all I could find."

"This is very helpful." Zoe tucked the photo back into the file. "Is there anything else you can tell me? Did anyone in particular admire the painting? Had anyone ever offered to purchase it from your family?"

"No." Poppy shrugged. "Nothing like that."

"Well, what can you tell me about it? Your family must have talked about it. Your mother is fond of it?"

"Yes, that's right. Very fond of it." She motioned to the chairs. "Won't you sit down? I'll tell you what I can, but it's not much. Mother has always loved it," Poppy said as they sat down. "That's why I called Uncle Harry. If it can be recovered, it would be the best thing. She's had such a shock recently."

"Harrington told me about your father. I'm sorry," Zoe said.

"Yes, that was incredibly hard." Poppy looked down and sucked in a deep breath.

"I'm sorry," Zoe repeated and wondered if she should offer to look for some tissues.

But Poppy pressed a hand to her mouth for a moment then

recovered her composure. "No, I'm the one who is sorry. Father's stroke was so sudden. Only a few weeks after it happened, he was gone." She blinked a few times. "Mother has decided to sell this place." Her gaze ranged over the gallery and down to the main room. "When the subject came up, the first thing mother mentioned was *A View of Edinburgh* and how she wants to hang it in the flat in London. Of course, when I realized it was gone I didn't mention it to her. She's rather... delicate...at the moment. If you can find the painting, I can take it back to her when I return to London in a few days. Do you think that will be possible?"

Poppy gazed at Zoe, a pleading look in her bulging eyes, but Zoe knew better than to make an outright promise. "I'll do everything I can to find it. Let's go through exactly what happened. Was it stolen while you were here? You don't live here full-time, do you?"

"No. I only came up on Monday to begin preparations to sell the house. That's when I found the broken window." Poppy had recovered from her weepy state, and now there was an edge of anger to her tone. Zoe could identify. When her house in Dallas had been broken into, Zoe had felt the same way. While Zoe could understand Poppy's emotional state, her words made Zoe's hopes of wrapping up this case quickly do a nose-dive. "So how long had the house been unoccupied?" Zoe asked.

"For several months. No one has been up here since, oh I don't know, probably November."

"So that painting could have been taken anytime between November and Monday?"

"Oh no. Everything was fine last Thursday. Mrs. Reid comes every Thursday to check the house and clean. She would have called if the window was broken. It had to have happened sometime between Thursday afternoon and when I arrived on Monday. Mrs. Reid always finishes by noon."

"Okay," Zoe said, feeling somewhat relieved. At least she could narrow down the time of the painting's disappearance to within the last week. "I'd like to talk to Mrs. Reid." Zoe opened her notebook and wrote down the name on the first pristine page.

"Of course." Poppy half-pushed off from the cushions, then dropped back down. "I don't have her phone number in my phone. She's just got a new mobile, and I don't have her new number with me, but I can get it for you."

"That would be good. Now, what about neighbors? Have you talked to anyone?"

Poppy reared back. "No, I haven't said a word to anyone, except Uncle Harry. Mother knows absolutely *everyone*. She's very social, and I didn't want to risk any whisper about the missing painting getting back to her." She gave a dismissive wave of the hand. "And it probably doesn't matter anyway." The house next door is for let. It's been empty an age, and the other closest building, the one that forms the nearest corner of the close, is under renovation. So, only workmen coming and going there."

"But someone might have seen something," Zoe said.

Poppy looked distressed. "Please, isn't there something else you can do? Some other thing you can focus on? I know talking to people around the close will be useless."

Zoe doubted that Mrs. Foley's social circle extended to the construction workers in a specific building in Edinburgh, but Zoe bent her head over her notebook and made a note on possible witnesses. She wasn't about to alienate Poppy. She was the client, after all. Zoe had learned through dealing with clients in her various temp jobs that the client might not always make the best choices and decisions, but the client was always right. At the end of the day, the client paid the bill. "We can hold off on that, for now. You do understand that Harrington has asked a local art dealer to put out the word that we're interested in the painting?"

"Yes. He explained that." Poppy didn't look happy. "I'd rather not do that either, but he said we didn't have a choice."

"That's true."

"And have you heard anything from the art dealer?" Poppy asked.

"No, but I met with her before I came here. I promise I'll contact you the moment I hear something." Zoe verified that she had her correct phone number then said, "Okay, so is there anything else you can think of that could help us?"

"No. I'm sorry, but I can't think of any reason someone would waste time and risk breaking in here to get a painting that only has sentimental value."

---

Ivan Barrows, Head of Special Collections at one of Edinburgh's finest institutions of higher learning, closed his eyes as his assistant, located at her desk outside his office door,

honked into yet another tissue. Ivan closed his laptop with a
snap. He'd leave work early today. He couldn't concentrate on
the department budget with all that sniffling and sneezing
going on mere feet from him. His glance slid to the tiny
window where a square of pale gray sky today had replaced
the usual square of dark gunmetal gray sky. The weather the
last few days had been horrendous—either solid sheets of rain
drumming straight down or sheets of rain blowing sideways. A
cold, cloudy day was an improvement.

He shrugged into his leather coat and wrapped his wool
Armani scarf around his neck. He packed his laptop and a few
files into his briefcase then turned off his office lights.

"You're leaving?" Alice Wicks asked from behind a tissue
she was using to swab her bright pink nose.

"I have an appointment."

"You don't have anything on your calendar."

"It's personal." Ivan strode away quickly as he called over
his shoulder, "Have a good weekend."

He trotted down the exterior steps of the library, drawing
in great breaths of the painfully chilly air, contemplating his
options. He could go home, of course, but all he had at home
was a tin of tomato soup and some stale bread, and his
stomach was rumbling for lunch. No, he'd head over to that
little antique shop on Prince's Street and get something to eat
on the way. He could look through that collection of books
that the owner had emailed him about. Stuart had tipped him
off to several nice finds in the past. It might be worth his time.

An hour later, Ivan sat at a card table, which sloped steeply
toward him, removing one dusty book from the cardboard box

at a time. A bell chimed as a customer entered the store, and the pimply kid who'd shown him to the table in the back room after getting the owner's approval via a phone call disappeared through the green velvet curtain into the front of the shop.

Ivan breathed a sigh of relief. The constant chimes, bells, and other miscellaneous clanging sounds from the kid's phone had been so distracting that Ivan had to look through one stack twice to make sure he hadn't missed a gem. Stuart was out of the shop, and Ivan decided to always make sure the owner was in, if he returned to check a shipment.

Ivan reached back into the box for the next book. These were all run-of-the-mill. Average. Yes, they were old books, but that wasn't enough to tempt him. He had found a nice manuscript of medieval poetry in this shop not too long ago— that was why Stuart had called him with the offer to look through the books—but Ivan had a feeling that lightning wasn't going to strike today in the form of an overlooked rare book.

Ivan heaved the last box onto the table. The kid returned to the back room and began banging things about on a little counter. "Like a cuppa?"

"No." Ivan flung the flaps of the box back, and dust spun into the air.

"Sure?"

Ivan gripped the edge of the box, his head tilted to the side as he cut his gaze toward the teen's back. "Yes. Quite sure."

The teen shrugged and slapped a cabinet door closed.

Ivan let out a bellow-like sigh, but the teen didn't take the hint. Ivan pressed his eyes closed and gave a tiny shake of his head, wishing he'd brought his earbuds. He could have plugged them in and lost himself in something soothing, like Mendelssohn's *Andante* from his *Violin Concerto*. Even that ham-fisted ignoramus of a kid would have understood to leave him alone if he saw the cords trailing down from earbuds. It was probably the only thing he would understand since Ivan's sharp, one-syllable replies had not been enough to stem the continual flow of words aimed in his direction.

More words eddied around him, but Ivan ignored them, working his way through the box. Down at the bottom, he found what looked like a rather promising weathered leather cover, and he thought for a second it might be a Jansenist binding, but it was only a trick of the light. The volume turned out to be a group of proceedings from a forgotten building society that had been bound together. Ivan tossed the book back in the box then began to carelessly pitch in the other books that he'd already removed, humming the Mendelssonh's music under his breath.

The uncoordinated youth had finally succeed in making his tea and had now seated himself only inches away from Ivan, his words running on, despite the warm tea in the cup he held. A few words penetrated through Ivan's humming and thud of books falling into the box.

"...stolen painting...Annabel Foley—"

Ivan's hands stilled for a second as he ran the name around in his mind. Annabel. Yes, that had been the name. One of them anyway, that Poppy had nattered on about all those summers ago. Annabel Foley. Not exactly a common name. Memories stirred of a summer spent searching every nook and cranny at Frampton. Ivan picked up a book and slowly placed it in the box. "A painting, you said?"

The kid had been about to sip his tea, but he immediately lowered his cup. "Yes. Very important." He dug in his pocket and removed his phone. "Here, would you like to see?"

Ivan took the phone and stared at the small image, a landscape of Edinburgh. He didn't recognize it, but then again, Frampton had been covered in art, and at that point in his life, he'd paid little attention to it. He was about to hand the phone back when he noticed the line of text under the image, "*A View of Edinburgh* by Annabel Foley, ca. 1850."

The words he and Robbie had repeated over and over echoed around in his mind. They had peeked behind pictures, looked behind all the books in the library, and opened every door to every wardrobe until the housekeeper ordered them outside in frustration. *Surely the answer to the riddle couldn't be that simple...could it?*

"And this was stolen? From Frampton?" he asked. Why would inquiries about this painting be going out all the way up here in Edinburgh?

"Frampton? No, mate, it was stolen from a house in one of the closes off the Royal Mile. Stair something."

*Perhaps it was that simple*, after all. He'd need to find his notes, to see if it was possible, but it might just be. He felt a bubble of elation he got when he spied an especially nice book that had been overlooked and left forgotten on a shelf, and he was able to pluck it from among the inconsequential rabble.

It could be true. He would have to check, but that was easily done. He still had all his notes, all the research. It would be fittingly poetic if he actually found it, considering it was that object that had launched him into his current career. Yes, very fitting indeed.

He handed the phone back. "Has it been found?" he asked, interrupting the youth, who was rambling on again about some other nonsense.

He shrugged. "Don't know. I suppose not, or I would have heard."

"Well, can you find out?" Ivan gestured impatiently at the phone.

"Ah, I guess so."

"Then get on with it."

The kid frowned at him, but tapped out a text as Ivan worked his arms into the sleeves of his coat and wrapped his scarf around his neck. The phone let out a stream of music, which the kid cut off as he clicked to the text. "Nope, still missing."

"Excellent," Ivan murmured. "If it comes in, call me," he said, and began dictating his phone number.

"Why?"

"So I can buy it," Ivan said, spacing out each word.

"Oh, right." But the kid looked uncertain. "You heard me say that it's stolen, right?"

"After the legalities are worked out, of course," Ivan said.

Once Ivan was sure the kid had his phone number, and he'd impressed on him that there would be an ample reward for calling him first before he called Stuart should the painting turn up, he left the shop. He had memorized the number that

the image had been texted from, and as he walked down the
street, he dialed the number.

"The Blue Door, how may I help you?"

Ivan smiled and hung up without speaking. He knew the
place. He'd go there, but first he needed to go home and dig a
box out of the back corner of a closet.

## 4

Z OE WALKED SLOWLY ACROSS JOHN'S Close, studying the surrounding buildings. The one immediately next door to Staircase House did indeed have a sign in the window proclaiming it was "To Let."

Zoe walked on, thinking about the minuscule differences there were between American English and British English. In America, that sign would have read, "To Rent." She'd also noticed on the drive from the airport that the words "Give Way" instead of "Yield" were printed on a triangular road sign. As interesting as it was to think about the points where a common language branched and split, vocabulary wasn't her top concern right now.

She turned and looked at the next closest building. Scaffolding lined one side, and swaths of plastic covered the upper floors. The main entrance was firmly shut. Zoe didn't see any workmen. So, no one to chat with, which was probably a good thing since she had promised Poppy she wouldn't talk to anyone around John's Close. If the art dealers were a dead end, she would ask Poppy to reconsider her ban on talking to the people in the neighborhood.

She turned to the buildings on the other side of the close, the taller stuccoed buildings of five- and six-stories. That would be a job, knocking on doors in those apartments and offices, but she wouldn't attempt it today. Zoe walked through the little tunnel, emerged onto the Royal Mile, and headed back to the hotel. It was time to have that conversation with Harrington and do some Internet research of her own.

She returned to the hotel, and checked the safe. The cash was still tucked away in the envelope. She closed the thick door and decided to do her Internet searches first. She spent about an hour combing through search results, looking for any mention of the painting. Harrington preferred to do things the old-fashioned way, like the handwritten note and paper currency, and she wanted to make sure she had all the bases covered, like the possibility that the Internet could be a sales point.

The search term of the painting's name turned up a few other paintings, but most of those had some sort of extra identification tagged onto the title, like "from the West" or "Castle." Zoe did find one painting online with the exact title, but it was a completely different painting attributed to another artist, and currently located in a museum collection, to boot. Violet would have been happy to see that the female artist was credited in the description of the painting.

Zoe found mentions of and quite a few links to Annabel's later works, her botanical studies, but the Internet only had a few links to the landscapes painted early in her career, and none of those were of the painting Zoe was interested in. Annabel's sister Agatha, who was also a great traveler, came up in the searches. Later in her life, Annabel had accompanied her sister on some international trips, using the opportunity to paint flora in places like the Mediterranean and Africa.

Zoe stood and paced around the room, rolling her head to stretch her neck as she picked up her phone.

Harrington answered on the second ring. "Zoe, my dear, how are you? Do you have everything you need? Is your room comfortable?"

"Yes, everything is fine."

"You received my package?"

"Yes. It's in the safe at the moment. Unfortunately, I don't know if I'll need it. Violet is a lovely woman, but I'm not sure she has the sort of connections we need..."

"Oh don't let that polished exterior fool you. Violet knows her stuff. It has only been a few days."

"But the longer we wait, the colder the trail gets."

"Very true. Is there something there, some lead you discovered that you can follow up on immediately?"

"No." Zoe sighed. "The next logical thing to do is talk to people in and around John's Close, but when I met with Poppy, she insisted that I *not* talk to anyone around John's Close, in case word somehow got back to her mother."

"Then we have to respect her wishes...for now."

Zoe smiled. "So wait then bring up the subject again, if we don't have anything else to go on?"

"Yes, that's how I would handle it."

Zoe was glad to hear those words. Harrington was good at this, and if her instincts were matching up with his, then she was probably doing okay. Buoyed by this confirmation, Zoe said, "I've thought of someone else who may be able to help us, an art dealer in Paris, Henry Masard."

Harrington said slowly, "Yes, Masard might be useful."

"You know him?" Zoe asked. It wasn't surprising when she thought about it. Harrington's work had taken him all over the world. She should have assumed Harrington and Masard would know each other.

"Years ago," Harrington said. "He helped me recover a nice little Degas bronze. I've kept in touch. Yes, that might be a good idea. I'll leave it up to you."

He asked a few more details about the meeting with Poppy, but his questions focused more on Poppy's state of mind than how Zoe had handled the interview. He simply wanted to make sure the daughter of his old friend was doing okay.

"She was a little nervous at first," Zoe said, "but that's understandable after a robbery."

"Yes. And some people are uncomfortable with the idea of hiring a recovery consultant. It's not something people do every day. Well, it sounds as if you're off to a good start. Call me if you need me. Shall we talk again tomorrow? Is this a good time?"

They arranged the time for the call the next day and hung-up. Zoe found Masard's number in her contact list— Harrington wasn't the only person who kept up with old acquaintances. The call went straight to voicemail where she listened to a stream of French that she didn't understand. At the sound of the beep, she left him a message in English.

She plopped down on the bed and drew the laptop toward her. Zoe couldn't sit around and wait. Waiting was not her strong suit. Jack was the one with all the patience. Zoe pulled up a map of Edinburgh and searched for antique stores and art galleries. She would visit as many of these herself as she could before jet lag got to her, then she'd hit the remainder in the morning.

She had her list and was putting on her knit cap in preparation to leave—the sun, behind the wall of mist and thin clouds, was completely down, and the temperature would have dropped—when her phone rang.

She recognized Violet's number.

"Good news, Zoe." The excitement in her tone brought out more of Violet's Scottish brogue. "We've found it."

## 5

VIOLET CONTINUED, "I JUST GOT off the phone with a dealer—a good friend of mine. She's actually in Glasgow. Her daughter ran her shop for her today and didn't know about the painting. Nancy only found out about it a few minutes ago when her daughter mentioned it."

"Wonderful. What's the address? I'll go pick it up right now."

"Oh no, you can't do that. Her daughter's already closed up the shop and gone home. She has two little ones, you see. But Nancy has an appointment here in Edinburgh tomorrow. She'll drop it off with me first thing tomorrow."

"Umm...I don't know about that. I don't like the idea of it sitting in a shop all night." Now that she knew where it was, Zoe wanted the painting in her possession. "I don't mind going to get it now. How far is Glasgow? This Nancy might have left a key with a neighbor or another shopkeeper. Could you ask her?"

"No, I don't think she does that. She's quite particular about her shop, and she wants to see it as well as bring it to you herself. And I can see why, too. It's a stolen painting, don't you know. She wants to be exactly sure of who she's turning it over to."

"And you'll vouch for me, I get it," Zoe said.

"Don't worry. It will be safe as houses overnight. You'll have it first thing tomorrow."

Zoe thought, *what did that even mean? Safe as houses?* Houses weren't always safe...Staircase House was a recent prime example of that. But it didn't appear that she'd be able to do anything about getting the painting tonight. She'd have to trust Violet, who had been as good as her word. She'd had the contacts to find the painting, so Zoe decided not to press.

"Okay. What time should I come by in the morning?"

"Eight too early?"

"No, I'd be there at five, if you said that was the best time."

Violet laughed. "Five is far too early for *me*. Now you can relax and enjoy your evening. Have you seen the castle? You must do that."

They said good-bye, and Zoe folded the list of galleries and antique shops in half then tossed it in the wastepaper basket, feeling a bit...let down, she realized. After all the worry and venting to Jack about what *she* would do to find the painting, what resources *she* could bring to the table, what innovative ways *she* could come up with to find the painting...and all she had needed to do was come to Edinburgh, and wait for it to be handed to her. *Oh well, nothing like a little lesson in humility*, Zoe thought.

She brought up Poppy's phone number, but hesitated before typing a text or calling. She closed the screen. Zoe decided to wait until she had the painting in hand before she got in touch with Poppy. Instead, she called Harrington. Text messages were not his thing. He didn't answer, so she left him a voice message, updating him on what had happened. "I'll have Violet look at it," Zoe said. "I think she's as close to an expert as we're going to get with Annabel Foley's paintings." During the last few months, she and Harrington had developed a protocol for dealing with recovered items. Once they recovered an item, their next step was to verify that the item was actually authentic, a step which might prove difficult as there was so little known about Annabel Foley's early work, but Violet had seemed extremely knowledgeable. "Let me know if there is someone else you'd rather I use for the verification," Zoe said. "I'll get in touch with you tomorrow after I have the painting."

She grabbed her room keycard and headed for the rainbow elevator. She had time on her hands and a foreign city to explore. Might as well see the castle before jet lag forced her to sleep.

---

Ivan dragged another box from the recess of his closet and checked the contents. *Finally*, he thought, spotting a notebook wedged deep in a corner. He added it to the pile of books on the table beside his laptop. It had taken him longer to find what he was looking for than he'd anticipated. All his research was not in the same box. At some point, he'd moved things around, and it had taken him several hours to sort through his cluttered closet. But he had it all spread out in front of him now. He sat down, opened the notebook, and set to work, going back and forth between his old research notes and the goldmine of information that was the Internet.

After two hours, he fell back in his chair, disgusted. He was on the right track. He knew it. He could feel it. The information was lining up in a way it never had before, but he needed that painting. He couldn't believe that there wasn't a photo of it anywhere on the Web. How could that be? He understood it wasn't one of Annabel Foley's famous botanicals, but it was part of her body of work.

He picked up his phone again. He knew he hadn't received a message from the kid at the antique store. He couldn't have missed an incoming call or a text. The phone had been within arm's reach, volume turned up as high as it would go. He sent another text then pushed away from the table. It was too late to go to the Blue Door. It would probably be closed now, but he could go anyway, see if the owner was working late. Maybe charm his way into some more information about the painting.

He shrugged into his coat and was reaching for his keys when his phone rang. Ivan recognized the number. It was the antique shop he'd been in earlier.

The owner's voice came over the line when he answered. "Mr. Barrows, this is Stuart. So sorry I missed you today. Timothy informed me you're expanding into oils, and that you'd like a landscape."

"Yes, the painting your employee described today sounded like exactly what I'm looking for."

A second of silence filled the line then Stuart said, cautiously, "Tim mentioned it, did he?"

"Yes. I'm actually friends with the family of the woman who painted it," Ivan said. "I'd like to acquire it...to return it to the family, of course. I know the son, Robert, quite well."

"I wish I could help you, but the painting is already in the process of being returned to the family at Staircase House."

"Ah, I see," Ivan said. "Well, that's—good. Excellent, in fact. Glad that's sorted," Ivan said. "Did you see it? Did it come into your shop?"

"Oh, no. I just got the word, a text, that it had been found. Not sure where it turned up. Now, I do have a nice little Victorian oil, a seascape—"

"Yes, of course. I'll take a look at it next time I'm in. Thank you. Appreciate the call." Ivan hung up and paced around the room, still in his coat. *In the process of being returned.* What did that mean? Was it on the way back to Staircase House? Was it there already? Stuart had said it was being returned to Staircase House itself. That meant someone had to be there to receive it.

He moved back to the table and found the list of numbers he'd jotted down inside the notebook's front cover years ago. With any luck the numbers wouldn't have changed. He found the number for Staircase House and dialed.

After three rings, a female voice said, "Hello?"

*Poppy.* Instinctively he pushed the end button. Even after all these years, he could still hear her snobby tones ringing out as she called him Ivan the Terrible in a voice that carried all the way down the grand staircase and into the long hall at Frampton.

He ran his hand over his mouth, trying to come up with another way to do things, but there wasn't any other way. He had to call Robert. There was no way Poppy would let him in Staircase House, much less let him see the painting.

———————

Zoe was not normally a morning person. Unlike Jack who was disgustingly cheerful, she usually needed at least an hour and a few cups of coffee to become even slightly coherent. But even with the time change, she had woken at six and thrown back the covers, not even thinking of grabbing a few extra minutes in the warm bed. By seven-thirty she was walking along the cobblestoned crescent toward the Blue Door. She knew she was early, but she couldn't help it. She would check and see if Violet was in. Violet might be an early bird type person.

But when Zoe arrived at the shop, the royal blue door was locked and the interior lights were off. A sign posted near the door showed that Violet normally opened at ten. Zoe walked on until she found a bakery where she purchased a coffee and a chocolate croissant, which she ate, perched at a cafe table on the sidewalk. She had her choice of tables. The morning was clear, but chilly, and there weren't many people lingering at the cafe tables over breakfast. Zoe was bundled for the weather in her gloves, hat, and scarf, but she finished her food quickly and went back to walking to stay warm, heading back to the shop.

By eight, she was again back in front of the store, which was still locked. Her phone rang. Zoe saw it was Violet's number, and her heart sank. Something had gone wrong.

"Good morning, Zoe." Violet's chirpy tone reassured Zoe somewhat. "Change of plans, I'm afraid. Nancy has had to delay her departure from Glasgow until later this morning. She will be here by eleven, so I'll see you then."

"You know, I think I should just go there." Zoe didn't like all this waiting around for the painting and depending on someone's schedule.

"Oh, no need to do that. She's already left, but she has to make a couple of stops on the way, so the painting wouldn't even be there, if you made the trip. Just have a nice relaxing morning. See you soon."

Zoe blew out a breath and put her phone away. Nothing she could do about it now, but the thought of this Nancy person carting the painting around central Scotland as she ran her errands didn't fill Zoe with confidence. She should have insisted on going after it last night. Zoe shook her head. Jack wouldn't believe this when she told him. She'd never been too timid. It wasn't like her. She was more a barrel-ahead kind of girl than pause-and-contemplate-the-consequences kind of girl. She'd never been too timid before, but she had hesitated this time and gone with Violet's plan. She wouldn't let that happen again, but there was nothing she could do about it now.

She dug her hands into her pockets. Since she was waiting

it out, she would see some more of Edinburgh. At least sight-seeing might make the time pass faster. She ran through her options. She knew from her trip to the castle last night that it didn't open until nine-thirty. She'd also learned that it closed at five. She'd missed the last entrance so she had gone to the National Gallery of Scotland instead. She'd spent the majority of her time in the Impressionist rooms, checking out paintings by Monet and his colleagues, but as she'd wandered through the galleries, she'd spotted paintings by Gainsborough, Titian, Constable, van Gogh, and even a da Vinci. It had been nice and toasty warm inside the museum, too, which was a bonus.

With the sun shining down this morning, it didn't feel as cold as it had last night, but her breath sent little puffs of white into the air as she made her way through the city. It was early, so she ambled, stopping to browse in shop windows as she crossed the Royal Mile and continued on to Princes Street Gardens, the area that had once been a lakebed. Zoe paused at the top of a set of stairs. The ground sloped down, creating a narrow trough-like area.

Buildings, bridges, and even a train station dotted the scooped out landscape. The museum she'd visited last night was located there, on the Mound, a central area where construction debris had been dumped when the elegant lanes of the "new town" on the other side of the gardens and Princes Street were being built in the late 1700s. Last night, a Ferris wheel in the gardens had been lit up, drawing her attention to its bright lights, but now in daylight she took in the whole view, wondering if Annabel Foley had ever painted the scene at night.

She trotted down the steps and through the park to the towering gray-toned monument to Sir Walter Scott. She figured that this early in the morning it was the most viable tourist site to visit. It was hard to close an open-air monument. From a distance, the monument had looked dark, nearly black, but as she got closer, she saw that some of the stones were a golden-brown tone, and she wondered if the darker stone near the top was due to pollution or some other chemical reaction...maybe something similar to copper turning green over time. She cranked her neck back to take in all 200-feet of the wonder with its gothic arches and protruding gargoyles.

She remembered from her copyediting days that someone had called it a "gothic rocket ship," and she agreed. A statue of Scott, seated with a book in his hand and his dog at his side, was centered up under all the architectural extravagance and looked quite humble compared to the massive enclosure. The viewing platforms were closed, but she wasn't in the mood to climb the 287 steps. Instead, she settled into a restaurant and ordered a full breakfast. She burned enough time lingering over her coffee that by the time she retraced her steps, the castle was open.

She bought a ticket and passed through an arched entry with the sharp points of the lower edge of the metal gate hanging just in sight overhead. Zoe toured the tiny rectangular St. Margaret's Chapel, the oldest building in Edinburgh, her guidebook informed her. She ducked her head as she stepped into the building that had been constructed in 1130, thinking what a hearty people the Scottish had been—not a fireplace in sight in the bare room. Next, she crossed the threshold into the reverent atmosphere of the Scottish National War Memorial. The alcoves with books listing the names of men who had died in battles from World War I onward saddened her as she thought of all those lives cut short by war.

She moved on to the royal palace and, while the rooms were not as opulent as some other grand homes she'd toured in Europe, she thought the low-key rooms perfectly in keeping with the image of Scotch frugality. Then she had a look at the crown jewels, which interestingly included a rough stone rectangle, which Scottish kings were seated on during their coronations until the English took it away in the 13th century. It was displayed in the same case as the crown, scepter, and sword. She would have enjoyed the whole thing more, if she hadn't been constantly checking the time.

By the time she emerged from the gate, it was finally ten-thirty, and she headed back to the Blue Door, stopping by the hotel on the way to remove the money from the safe. A price hadn't been discussed, but Zoe assumed she was going to have to buy the painting from Nancy. Presumably, Nancy had purchased it from the person who had brought it into her shop. Zoe figured she'd at least need to reimburse her for that expense.

This time when she arrived at the Blue Door, the lights were on inside. She heard two female voices as she pushed through the door, which jangled the set of bells. Violet's head appeared over the top of the louvered door. "Zoe, come in. We're back here."

Violet made the introductions as Zoe squeezed into the

tiny space, her back pressed against the louvered doors. Nancy, a woman with a pudgy figure and a short crop of iron gray curls, reached for the brown paper wrapped package, which was propped up by her foot. Zoe breathed a sigh of relief at the sight of the package.

"Here you are. Is this it?" Nancy said, handing it to Zoe.

She folded back the paper to reveal a small oil painting. The painting and the frame looked like the photograph Poppy had given her, but she handed it off to Violet as she said, "At first glance, I think it is." Zoe removed the larger photograph and handed it to Violet. "You know Annabel Foley's work better than I do. Would you say this is the stolen painting? Harrington said you'd be the one to ask about that." He'd called her back last night, confirming that Violet was the person to check the painting.

One of Violet's hands fluttered to her hair. "Harrington said that? Well, that's kind of him."

"Yes, he said you were the perfect person for the job, in fact."

"Oh, I don't know about that," Violet said, but her tone said she was pleased. She positioned the painting on the desk, took the photograph from Zoe, and removed a magnifying glass from a drawer then leaned over the painting, comparing it to the photo.

"I don't know what all the fuss is about." Nancy had picked up a teacup from the corner of Violet's desk. She leaned back, propping her saucer on her midsection. "Nothing special about that painting. Why someone would take the trouble to steal it, I have no idea."

Zoe thought of the botanical paintings that had bracketed it and wondered if a mistake had been made. "It has sentimental value to the family," Zoe said. "Maybe the thief took the wrong painting."

Nancy snorted. "What kind of thief doesn't know what is valuable and what isn't? Not much of a thief, or not a very good one, at any rate."

"Who brought it into the shop?" Zoe asked as Violet continued to move back and forth between the painting and the photo.

"A man, but I didn't see him. My daughter talked to him. She's worked with me for years and knows that we can move a nice Victorian landscape of Edinburgh, which is what she told the man. She didn't know about the email Violet had sent. I didn't think of telling her." Nancy slid her saucer onto the desktop and linked her fingers together over her protruding stomach. "He must have taken it to several shops because she said he didn't seem surprised about the assessment. More resigned, she called it. Anyway, he said, 'Fine. I'll take it,' and she paid him for it."

"Did you get his name?"

"Oh yes, we keep records." She removed a slip of paper from the table and handed it over.

"Bob Roberts?" Zoe read in disbelief. In Scotland, a man named Roberts would be as difficult to find as a man named Smith in the States.

Nancy's eyes glinted with mischief. "An alias, no doubt, but it is the name he gave."

"What about a description?"

"She didn't remember much. She thought he was in his thirties. Medium height, brown eyes and wearing a dark wool coat and driving cap. Plaid scarf. Green and blue," Nancy added with a nod as if that last detail would separate the anonymous man from thousands of other men in Scotland.

"Nothing remarkable about him? A birthmark? Facial hair?"

"No, I believe my daughter said he was clean-shaven, but nothing stood out. No tattoos or scars or anything. She said he looked like a prosperous, law-abiding citizen. Quite shocked, she was when I told her about the missing painting. 'But mum, I took in one like that today,' she said, her eyes as big as saucers."

"Did he say how he came to have it?"

"He *said* it had been in his family for years, but we hear that all the time, don't we, Violet?" Violet murmured an agreement then looked up.

"I think it is the same painting. I'm not one-hundred percent sure, but the signatures are the same, and the brush-strokes that are visible in the photograph match the painting." She handed Zoe the magnifying glass, and they shuffled around, changing positions so that Zoe could lean over the painting and compare it to the photograph.

Violet pointed out the similarities, then said, "Even the frame appears to be the same." In the photograph, she pointed to a scratch on the lower right-hand side of the simple wooden frame then touched the frame where a similar line marred the wood.

Zoe straightened and handed the magnifying glass back to

Violet with a smile. "Looks like I can return *A View of Edinburgh* to Poppy Foley today."

They changed places again. As Violet wrapped the painting in the brown paper, Zoe turned to Nancy. "So, how much do I owe you for the painting?"

Nancy tilted her head to one side. "If it had been one of the botanicals, it would be harder to part with, but seeing as it's not...two-hundred and fifty pounds will cover the painting and transport here."

"Fine." Zoe hadn't been sure what sort of number to expect, and she'd been prepared to argue for a lower price if Nancy asked for some exorbitant figure, knowing as she did now that the Foley landscapes weren't worth as much as her paintings of flowers and plants. While two-hundred and fifty might be a little on the high side, Nancy had contacted Violet and brought the painting to Edinburgh.

Zoe handed over the pound notes. Nancy tucked them into a pocket on her tweed jacket. "I'll need a receipt. Since it was stolen."

"Of course." Zoe borrowed some paper from Violet, making a mental note to create some sort of official receipt form before her next job, and hand-wrote a receipt for Nancy.

Within a few minutes, Zoe was out the door, the little brown bundle tucked away in her messenger bag. First, she called Harrington with an update, then she dialed Poppy. She didn't answer, so Zoe left a message. "Hi, Poppy. Excellent news. I have the painting. I'll drop by Staircase House on my way back to the hotel in case you get this. If not, I can return it this afternoon."

She checked the time, then called Jack. "I have it," she said as soon as he answered.

"I can't say I'm surprised. So the other dealer showed up?" Jack had called Zoe last night during a break at the conference, and she'd told him about Nancy bringing the painting.

"Yes, finally. She was delayed this morning. I had to wait until eleven to pick it up."

"That must have been rough. Waiting a whole three extra hours must have been torture."

Zoe heard the teasing tone in his voice. "Yes, it was awful. So bad that I had to take myself to the castle to get my mind off it. I'll tell you about it later. I'm almost to Staircase House. I'll call you back with all the details after I return it."

"Sounds good. I have a session in fifteen minutes than I'm all yours."

"I like the sound of that. Too bad we're on different continents." Zoe's words echoed a bit as she walked through the tunnel arch into John's Close.

"You're wrapping up there and will be home soon. You might even beat me home."

"It's possible." They said good-bye and Zoe reached for the doorbell of Staircase House, which looked like a modern addition to the aged house.

After a few moments, a dark-headed woman that Zoe hadn't seen before opened the door.

"Hi," Zoe said. "I'm looking for Poppy Foley. Is she in?"

The woman's elegant eyebrows snapped down into a frown. "I'm Poppy. Do I know you?"

## 6

THE WOMAN STOOD IN THE dim recess of the stair's landing, the contrast between the bright light outdoors and the shadowy interior making it difficult to see her, but Zoe could see enough to know that this was not Poppy.

"I said, do I know you?" The woman repeated, her tone implying that she didn't think she did, and if she had made Zoe's acquaintance it had certainly been a mistake.

When Zoe had pressed the bell, she'd lifted the flap of her messenger bag and she had been in the process of reaching for the painting, but she pulled her hand away now and let the flap fall back into place. Perhaps the woman had misunderstood her and thought she said something other than the name "Poppy." Zoe had dealt with a lot of different types of people in her freelance job-juggling days, and she recognized this woman's approach: sheer intimidation mixed with distain, a combination that probably gave her the upper hand with most people right off the bat. But Zoe wasn't most people, and she'd had plenty of experience dealing with rather inconsiderate people. Zoe put on a determined smile and enunciated her words carefully. "No, I don't believe we've met. I'm Zoe Andrews. Are you sure Poppy Foley isn't here? I spoke with her here yesterday."

The woman let out a little half-laugh that didn't involve her mouth, but did make her shoulders twitch. "Here? You met her here?"

"Yes."

"Well, that's impossible. I'm Poppy Foley, and since I was in London most of yesterday, I certainly didn't meet you here."

A bit of Zoe's confidence seeped away, and doubt nibbled at the edge of her thoughts. *I only have this woman's word that she's Poppy,* Zoe thought. *But, then again, the woman I met yesterday had only given me her word as well.*

The woman was about to close the door, so Zoe stepped forward and put her hand on the doorframe. "Well someone met me here yesterday. She unlocked the door, invited me in, and said she was Poppy Foley."

The woman narrowed her eyes at Zoe. "Why would someone do that?"

Zoe tried to take a deep breath without being obvious about it. "I can't tell you that until you show me some proof that you are Poppy Foley. If you are—"

Zoe broke off as the woman rolled her eyes and muttered, "Really, the nerve—"

"If you are Poppy," Zoe continued, "you will want to know what it was about."

For a second, Zoe thought the woman would slam the door

on her fingers, but she threw open the door instead, and motioned Zoe up the stairs in front of her. "Fine."

She closed the front door and followed Zoe up the curving staircase. Zoe scanned the room. It looked the same as yesterday, except the little table near the door where they'd left their purses and the bag of food was bare except for a set of keys. The woman went to a Chesterfield sofa positioned across from the gigantic fireplace. She leaned over and snatched up a supple leather handbag. She extracted a wallet with a designer logo on the catch, flipped it open, and held it out toward Zoe like a police officer showing a badge.

The words "Poppy Anna Foley" were printed beside a picture that made her clear skin look sallow. Zoe closed her eyes briefly. *What was going on?*

The woman—Poppy, Zoe thought distractedly. *This* was Poppy Foley—snapped the wallet closed, tossed it along with the purse onto the sofa, and crossed her arms. "Now. What is going on?"

"That's what I'd like to know," Zoe said.

"Why don't you start with why you came here in the first place? You're American, I can tell by your accent. Why are you in Edinburgh?"

Now that she'd mentioned accents, it registered that Poppy's accent was quite a bit more posh than the accent the woman had spoken with yesterday—the fake Poppy, no, that sounded too weird—the impostor, Zoe decided as she rubbed her forehead. Besides her slightly more upper-class speech, Zoe saw that everything about this woman spoke subtly of wealth. There were certain obvious signs: her sweater, which although it was casual, was made of a soft cashmere, and her leopard loafers were Louboutin—her friend Helen had snapped up a pair just like them on an eBay auction. Her short brown hair was styled away from her perfectly made-up face in short silky waves that ended at her strong jawline and emphasized the dimple in her chin. There was something else, too. She had an unmistakable air of confidence and self-assurance that rolled off her in waves.

"It's about a painting," Zoe said, knowing she had to tread carefully. "A painting that was stolen from your family."

Poppy's gaze zipped over Zoe's head and up to the gallery. "The landscape?"

"Yes."

"A woman hired my firm to find it. We did." Zoe took the brown paper bundle out of her messenger bag and handed it to Poppy.

She didn't bother to unfold the wrapping carefully. She ripped it away, revealing a corner of blue sky and part of the city below. "I'm calling the police."

***

Robert Foley picked up the post from the mat and tossed it face down onto an already tilting stack of mail so that he couldn't see the red notices stamped on the envelopes. He paced to the plate glass window that enclosed the living room and looked at the city. How much was this view worth? If he sold the flat, would it be enough to stop the arrival of more envelopes with red letters stamped on the outside? Probably not. His phone rang, and he turned his back on the view, pacing quickly across the room to his makeshift desk, a folding chair positioned in front of two cardboard boxes.

He snatched up the phone, ready to launch into his pitch, but when he saw the name Ivan on the display, his shoulders sagged. What was Ivan doing calling him? It had been—what? —months? Maybe a year since they'd spoken. Ivan was probably in town. Last time he was in London, Robert had invited Ivan to meet him here at his flat. He'd just purchased the place and had wanted to show it off, but now...well, he wouldn't be inviting anyone up to tour his flat, not now.

The rooms were empty except for the boxes and the chair in the living room. Beyond the kitchen with its gleaming appliances with digital read-outs was a luxurious bath with one towel and an empty bedroom with a sleeping bag on the floor. Robert hit the button to send the call to voicemail, but less than a minute later Ivan's name was back on the display of the ringing phone.

Robert sighed and answered the call. Ivan was persistent. Robert would have to make some excuse to keep Ivan from coming to the flat. He was becoming quite an expert in deflection and evasion lately. Robert pulled out his heartiest tones. "Ivan, how are you?"

"Excellent. You're not going to believe this, but I think I've figured it out, the riddle about the Foley Cache."

It took Robert a few seconds to rearrange his thoughts. The Foley Cache. It had been years since he'd heard those words. They brought back memories of him and Ivan scouring every inch of Frampton, crawling in and out of dusty cupboards and tapping paneling as well as roaming over the grounds, looking for a conspicuous pile of dirt that might hold a treasure. Idiotic stuff, but entertaining when you're eight.

Ivan hurried into the silence. "I know you're quite the busy investor these days, and you probably think the Foley Cache is as obtainable as the pot of gold at the end of the rainbow, but I think I know where to begin. Something came to my attention lately. It made me realize that we—and everyone who has ever searched for it—has been looking at the riddle the wrong way."

"Ivan—" Robert broke off. He didn't even know where to start. "It's a complete fantasy," he said finally. "If some Victorian Foley did bring back something valuable from a Grand Tour it would have been found by now."

"No, it wouldn't. Everyone has been looking in the wrong place."

Robert paced to the huge window, stifling another sigh. A few months ago, he would have made some excuse and ended the call—he had important things to do. But now his most pressing engagement was with his unopened post. Might as well hear him out. He knew Ivan. Ivan would keep pestering him until he had the whole story out and felt convinced that he'd talked Robert around to his point of view. It had been the same with Ivan's love of Arsenal. He plagued Robert with facts, figures, and reports of the team's exceptional talents, until Robert finally agreed that, yes they were the best team just to get Ivan to shut up.

Robert strolled back to his "office" and dropped into the folding chair. He propped his feet up on a box. "So why has everyone been looking in the wrong place?" Lounging back in the chair, Robert picked up a mass of rubber bands layered to create a ball and idly tossed it up and down with his left hand.

"I'll tell you on one condition. I get twenty percent of the find."

"The find." Robert couldn't keep the laughter out of his voice. "Come on, Ivan. We're adults here."

"Yes. That's why I want this spelled out. I'll help you find the Foley Cache, but I get twenty percent. I've got a solid lead. I want everything in writing beforehand, so there aren't any arguments later. I have a contract with me now. Where would you like to meet to sign it? Should I come by your flat? Are you home?"

Robert caught the ball and didn't toss it again. "No, I'm not home," Robert said automatically, his mind racing. Ivan was a trained academic now. If he'd found...something...that could lead them to the Foley Cache...Robert's glance ranged around the echoing room then strayed to the stack of bills. "Ten. Ten percent." What did he have to lose? If Ivan was right, it could be the answer to all his problems. If he was wrong, well, it wasn't like he was doing anything else right now.

"Fifteen."

"Ivan, let's say by some crazy miracle we actually do find it. It's my family treasure. I'll have to split it with Poppy."

"Poppy is your problem, not mine, thank God. Fifteen or I hang up and pursue this on my own."

"Fine. Fifteen. Now what have you found out?"

"Not quite yet. First, we meet and you sign this contract I have, then I need a look at something in Staircase House."

"What?"

"A painting."

---

When Poppy said she was calling the police, Zoe had pressed down her first instinct, which was to push past Poppy and get out of the house. But while physically her body was poised for flight, intellectually she knew that would be the worst thing she could do. It would make her look guilty.

Poppy made a call on her cell phone then retreated to the far side of the room by the doorway near the circular staircase. Zoe wasn't sure if it was because she wanted to be able to get out of the house if Zoe made a move toward her, or if Poppy wanted to be near the door to let the police in the instant they knocked.

Zoe sat down on the Chesterfield and waited.

It was probably only about twenty or thirty minutes between the time Poppy called and when the police arrived, but sitting silently in a room with someone who thinks you are a thief made it seem much longer—like an eon or two. Finally, the police arrived, a man and a woman, both in black hats with checkerboard trim and bright yellow jackets dripping with gear attached to pockets and belts. "I'm Officer Donnelly," the man said, "with Officer Flint."

The minute the police cleared the threshold into the room, Poppy said, "There she is, the thief who stole the painting,"

Officer Donnelly took out a notebook and began asking Poppy questions, which she answered in an impatient tone while Officer Flint watched Zoe with a laser-like focus. Finally, Donnelly came across the room and pointed to the painting Poppy had placed on an end table by the sofa before making her phone call to the police.

"Yes. I'm sure her prints are all over it," Poppy said. "I only touched the wrapping paper." Poppy had moved closer as well, following the police officer.

Donnelly turned to Zoe. "And you are?" He took down her name and hotel information, then carefully examined her passport, noting down information from it before passing it to his partner. She took it and retreated to the entry area by the staircase, out of earshot.

"And what can you tell me about this painting?" Donnelly asked, drawing Zoe's attention away from his partner. Zoe felt vulnerable and exposed, watching the woman walk away with her passport.

"The firm I work for, Throckmorton Enquiries was hired to find it."

Poppy uncrossed her arms. "Uncle Harry is involved in this?" she said, her tone rising with disbelief. "No, that can't be. He'd never do something like this."

"Who is he?" Donnelly asked.

"Harrington Throckmorton," Poppy said. "He's a friend of the family. An upstanding man, who would *never* participate in a robbery."

"But he didn't, and neither did I," Zoe said quickly, thinking it was best to get her side of the story on the record as quickly as possible. She hadn't bothered arguing with Poppy earlier. Even if she could have convinced Poppy that she wasn't a thief, the police were already on their way.

"A woman contacted Harrington earlier this week, said she was Poppy Foley and that a painting had been stolen. She asked if he could get it back."

Officer Donnelly tilted his head slightly. "Why would she ask him that?"

"Because that's what he does." Zoe gave him Harrington's background then said, "I work for him as a consultant. He couldn't make it here himself. He's currently working with the Guardia Civil on a case." Throwing in that detail couldn't hurt. "I was to meet Poppy Foley here, at this address yesterday," Zoe said to Donnelly, watching his partner speak quietly into a radio or phone—Zoe couldn't tell which—as she flicked through the passport. "I came early but no one answered the door, so I returned later. I met a woman walking across the close toward the door to this house. I introduced myself then she unlocked the door with a key. I followed her in. She showed me where the painting had been and had a folder of information ready for me with a close-up of the missing painting and other details." Zoe removed the folder from her messenger bag and handed it to Donnelly.

"So you never asked for identification?" he asked.

"It didn't cross my mind to ask for it. She had a key, and she knew her way around the house. She did seem a bit nervous at a few points," Zoe admitted, "but I assumed it was because she'd been robbed."

Donnelly looked toward Poppy, who shook her head. "I know nothing about this fantasy she's making up."

"Check the window in the gallery. Two panes have been replaced recently." Poppy spun and trotted up the stairs to the minstrel's gallery, nearly running over Officer Flint, who was returning Zoe's passport to Donnelly. He tilted his head toward the stairs, and Flint followed Poppy. Zoe heard Flint stumble on the taller step, catch her balance, and then continue up the rest of the stairs with a muttered curse.

Donnelly looked through the file then tucked it under his arm. He was taking a breath to ask another question, when Poppy appeared at the railing overhead, her face white and her dark eyes snapping. "Those panes are new, but I refuse to believe this nonsense. She broke in—that's how she knows about the window and the stolen painting."

"Then why would I repair the window?"

Momentarily stumped, Poppy didn't say anything.

"And why would I return with the painting?" Zoe added.

Poppy snapped her fingers and rushed down the stairs as she said, "It's a fake. You repaired the window and were returning the fake painting today to replace the stolen one."

"Then why did I ring the doorbell?"

Now at the bottom of the stairs Poppy shrugged. "To make sure the house was empty, of course."

"That's not true," Zoe said, her gaze going back and forth between Poppy's angry features and Donnelly's impassive face. "Not true at all. I've told you what happened."

Officer Donnelly cleared his throat. Zoe wondered if he felt the interview was getting away from him. "How valuable is this painting, Ms. Foley?"

She swiveled to look at the painting, which was still on the end table, in a speculative way.

*She has no idea,* Zoe thought.

"In the big scope of things, not a lot," Zoe said quickly. "It's a nice oil by Annabel Foley, one of Ms. Foley's ancestors, but not worth thousands of dollars, —er pounds. I paid a Glasgow dealer two hundred and fifty pounds for it this morning. Nancy..."

Donnelly raised his notebook, and Zoe cast about for Nancy's last name, but it escaped her. Why hadn't she saved herself a copy of that receipt? More mental notes for her next assignment...if there *was* a next assignment. *This job was in shambles,* Zoe thought, cringing inwardly, already dreading the conversation she'd need to have with Harrington after she extricated herself from the police. "Violet Buchanan, the owner of the Blue Door, can confirm everything I've told you. The woman I bought the painting from is named Nancy. She's a friend of Violet's. She can put you in touch with Nancy. Violet knows her stuff when it comes to Annabel Foley paintings, and she thinks this is the real deal. Not incredibly valuable, but she thinks it is authentic."

Donnelly made a note then said, "Let's get back to the woman you met here. What did she look like?"

"She was shorter than me, around five feet tall, I'd guess. She had brown eyes, a long nose, and chin-length brown hair cut in a bob, sort of frizzy."

Poppy turned her head slowly toward Zoe, her eyes narrowed. "Did she have protruding, buggy eyes?"

It wasn't the kindest description, but it was rather accurate. "Yes, she did."

Poppy's attitude changed. She went from indignation to exasperation. Her shoulders, which had been tensed up, dropped and she growled, "Justine, what have you done now?"

7

"**Y**OU THINK YOU KNOW THE woman Mrs. Andrews described?" Officer Donnelly asked Poppy.

"Yes," she said with a reluctant sigh. "Justine Price."

Justine was a funny name for a thief, Zoe thought.

"I've known Justine for years. She's a friend from school," Poppy continued, "You know, one of those connections that is based more on being in constant, forced company in a certain setting rather than on any real affinity. I hadn't spoken to her for—oh I don't know, probably seven or eight years until I ran into her a few months ago in London."

Poppy ran her finger around one of the buttons of the tufted sofa. "My father recently had a stroke. He was a difficult patient. She'd trained as a nurse, and Father was so finicky, I thought that having Justine around might be the solution. She had visited Frampton several times during school holidays when we were younger, so Father knew her. I thought it might be helpful to have someone he was familiar with. That was one of his complaints—too many strangers in the house."

She sat down on the sofa, rearranging her hands in her lap. "She was a good nurse. Father liked her, but during that time, some things went missing. Small items. An antique silver bell, a necklace, a jade elephant figurine. The Foleys have always been collectors, and the house is littered with items from all over the world. I wanted to confront her. Mother was afraid she'd take it the wrong way and leave us, which would upset Father. I didn't agree, but I didn't challenge her," she said in a tight voice. "Then Father died." She swallowed and looked up at the ceiling for a moment. Zoe couldn't help but compare her manner to the woman she'd met yesterday—Justine, who had also sprinkled references to parents into their conversation and had also choked up at the mention of her "father's" death. But Justine had recovered quickly, Zoe remembered, moving the conversation briskly along to the painting. Zoe didn't doubt for a second that Poppy's grief was real, mostly because she looked like she wanted to snatch back the last few seconds. She looked extremely embarrassed that anyone had caught a glimpse of her misery.

Poppy shook her hair back from her face and said in a firm voice, "At any rate, I would not put something like this," she gestured to the painting, "past her. I couldn't prove she took those things from the house, but we haven't had any problems since she left."

"But why would she impersonate you, if the painting isn't that valuable?" Donnelly asked as Flint came down the stairs and rejoined us.

"I don't know. Knowing Justine, she probably bought into one of Father's crazy theories about the Foley Cache."

"Euros, you mean?" Donnelly asked.

"No. Cache with a 'ch'—you know, treasure." She rolled her eyes as she said the last word.

"Oh." Donnelly went to make a note then pulled his pencil back. "Could you clarify?" Donnelly asked doubtfully.

Poppy tossed her head and scooted to the edge of the seat. "It is nothing important. There's an old family story, or legend I guess, that my grandfather entertained us with when we were kids. Supposedly, one of our ancestors went on a Grand Tour and returned with the Foley Cache, but instead of spending it or displaying it, it was hidden. It's been lost ever since."

"A treasure?" Zoe asked.

"Yes, it's absurd, I know, but when you're eight...you tend to believe that it's possible that a chest of gold doubloons is hidden in the attic. Or you want to believe the stories, no matter how ridiculous. Some people, like Justine and my brother, Robert," she rolled her eyes, "refuse to understand that it's just a story, a fairy tale."

"But why steal a painting? It has nothing to do with a treasure...does it?" Zoe asked. She'd looked at the painting through the magnifying glass and hadn't seen anything special, but perhaps it was like those hidden pictures within a picture. You didn't see it unless you knew exactly what you were looking for.

"No, of course it doesn't have anything to do with a treasure." Poppy closed her eyes for a moment and shook her head. "At the end, my father had a lot of time on his hands. He couldn't get around very well, and he took to reading about our family history. He went on and on about the painting. I didn't pay much attention. 'The painting is key.' He kept repeating it, but at that point, he wasn't all there, mentally, so of course, I discounted it. He was rather fixated on it, so I'm sure Justine heard him. She must have believed him. For some reason she thought this painting was valuable." She pronounced the last word sarcastically and stood abruptly. "I'm sorry to have taken so much of your time, Officer Donnelly." She turned to Zoe. "And I'm sorry I accused you of being a thief. This is a family matter, and I hope we can put it all behind us." She waved her hand toward the door, indicating it was time for Zoe to make her exit.

"But it's not quite all in the family," Zoe said. "This Justine person did involve Harrington, and we haven't sorted that out yet."

"Oh, I don't think there's much to sort out. Justine saw an opportunity to make a 'quick buck,' as you say in the States. She came here in order to retrieve the painting—she's visited with me over a holiday once."

"So you think she broke the window?" We all startled a little and turned toward Flint, who hadn't spoken the whole time.

"Yes, obviously," Poppy said.

"But if she worked at your family's estate," Zoe said, "would it be possible that she could get the key to this house and make a copy? She had a key when I met with her."

"How many keys are there to Staircase House, Ms. Foley?" Donnelly asked.

"Several." Poppy flashed Zoe a look of dislike. "But what you describe wouldn't be possible. I'm sure you don't understand how houses like these are managed. The housekeeper at Frampton is in charge of the keys for that house. She doesn't have the keys to Staircase House."

"But you have a copy, right? Probably on your key chain." Poppy's frown deepened, and Zoe knew her words had hit home. "So why couldn't Justine have slipped the key off your key ring, have a copy made, then returned the key without you knowing during one of your visits to see your father? Or, couldn't she have done that with someone else who might have a key, like your mother? Or," Zoe's voice became excited as another thought struck her, "even your father. Surely he had a key to Staircase House. As Justine nursed him, she would have been in and out of his rooms constantly and probably alone there at times, too. What would stop her from taking his keys and making a copy, if she thought there was something valuable here?"

"No, that's impossible," Poppy said, but her tone was less forceful than it had been earlier.

"It fits with the repaired window upstairs." Zoe said. "Someone must have broken in before she arrived—that's why she called Harrington. The painting was *already* gone when she got here."

Poppy watched Zoe for a moment with a sulky expression, then said, "Fine. Maybe that's what happened. I don't know. Justine is exactly the manipulative type of person who would contact Harrington, pretending to be me, and recruit him to find the painting. She did meet him once when she came home with me during half-term. He was visiting my parents at the time. I'm sure she would have invented some excuse not to meet him face-to-face if he'd come in person. She would have suddenly become sick or something and sent him everything he needed by messenger or online. Anyway, it was a stroke of good luck for her that he had to send you."

Officer Donnelly asked, "And the window repair?"

"Justine probably had it fixed so it wouldn't be noticeable." Poppy said, grudgingly. "I don't like to think that she was able to get her hands on a set of keys, but I suppose it is possible. If she did accomplish that and arrived to find the window broken, she would have to get it repaired. Our cleaner, Mrs. Reid, comes once a week and she would have called me immediately if she found a window broken. Justine probably hoped that Mrs. Reid wouldn't notice the missing painting. It's not as if it is displayed in a prominent place. And I wasn't planning to come up here until next week, but I had a sudden opening in my schedule and decided to come earlier. It might have been a week or more before we realized it was gone." Poppy's voice changed, becoming brisk. "But this is pointless speculation, Officer. Yes, Justine obviously found a way in, but," Poppy sent a veneer of a smile in Zoe's direction, "thanks to Mrs. Andrews, we have it back. All's well that ends well. Thank you for coming out. I'm sorry to have taken your time." Poppy had begun walking toward the door as she spoke the last few words and since Donnelly was in her path, he fell back so that she didn't plow into him. After a second's hesitation, he moved toward the door as well, the quiet shadow of Flint following him.

"Thank you for returning the painting, Mrs. Andrews," Poppy said, "but now that everything is settled, I have things to do and must ask you to leave."

"But why was the painting stolen in the first place, and who took it before Justine could?"

"I have no idea, and I don't care," Poppy said. "I'm satisfied with the outcome. Now if you'll excuse me..." She gestured to the circular staircase.

Zoe slipped her messenger bag over her shoulder. If she refused to leave, Poppy would probably have the police escort her out. Zoe trouped down the spiral stairs behind the officers with Poppy on her heels. At the door, Poppy thanked the officers again and then said, "There's no need to do any further investigation, and I'm not interested in pressing charges, at the moment." She set a warning glance toward Zoe with her last words and closed the door.

Zoe spun toward Donnelly. "Is that it? Case closed?"

Zoe didn't like it. There were too many unanswered questions for her taste, not to mention the fact that as things stood now, the accusation of theft had been leveled at her and the record hadn't been set straight. If there was one thing Zoe was incredibly leery of, it was unanswered accusations. Those had come back to bite her in the past, and she wasn't about to let it happen again. And this time it wasn't just about her, either. She worked for Harrington. Any smear of her name also reflected on him and his new company as well.

"A report will be filed," Donnelly said, "and we will be on

the lookout for," he consulted his notes, "Justine Price." Flint must have turned down her radio when they were in the house because now a crackling of static mixed with words spoken too quickly for Zoe to understand poured out of one of the gadgets that made up her gear. She unclipped the receiver and spoke into it as Donnelly said to Zoe, "We have your hotel information. We'll be in touch, if we need you again."

"That's what I'm afraid of," Zoe muttered as they strode away, their radio sputtering.

---

"You'd think a woman with the name 'Poppy' would have a chipper, sunny sort of personality, wouldn't you?" Zoe flopped back on the pillow and closed her eyes. Tense and worried, the bright colors of her hotel room only aggravated her more. "She was about the least sunny person I've ever met."

"The important thing is that she didn't push the police to do anything. It's good she dropped it." Jack had been concerned when she told him what had happened. Despite being worried, Zoe had been glad to have Jack to talk with. It was wonderful to have someone who truly cared about what happened to her and worried about her if something went wrong. She had soaked up his concern, assured him she was fine and that he didn't need to get on the first flight to Edinburgh. But now that they'd established that she was okay and moved on to dissecting what actually happened, his reasonable tone was beginning to irritate her.

"But don't you see," Zoe said, "leaving those accusations hanging isn't a good thing. Surely, you understand that?"

"Of course, I do, and we'll deal with that. You've told Harrington, right?"

"Yes, I left him a message with all the details."

"Good. So when is your return flight? I get home tomorrow morning, so I can pick you up anytime."

Zoe's ticket was an open return because they hadn't been sure how many days it would take to find the painting. She sat up. "I can't leave now. I have to figure out why Justine hired us and make sure this 'you're a thief, oh wait—no you're not' is taken care of."

"You can do all that from here."

"I can get a lot more done here in Edinburgh. I need to go back and talk to Nancy. Despite what the police said, I don't think they're going to follow up very extensively about the painting. You know how it is with art crime—it always gets shuffled to the bottom of the stack. And this isn't even an important or valuable painting, so there's also that component. Why steal it in the first place?"

"Zoe..." Jack's gusty sigh came over the line. "You should come home. I'm telling you, those are things we can sort out from here. You have the opportunity to leave Scotland now, no questions asked. You should do it."

Jack's experiences had made him a bit touchy, especially about freedom of movement.

A sharp knock cut off Zoe's reply. "Hold on a minute. That's probably the maid. She was down the hall when I came in."

Zoe opened the door, but it wasn't the maid. A police officer—not Donnelly—stood there. This guy was younger and had dark hair and a thick five o'clock shadow, which along with his baggy eyes and tired face, made him look like he'd been up all night. "Zoe Andrews?"

"Yes," Zoe said cautiously, her heart thumping. Suddenly despite all she'd said to Jack just moments before she wished she were on a flight this second, jetting home.

"If you could come with me, the inspector has some questions he'd like to ask you."

## 8

THE OFFICER AT HER HOTEL door had said the interview was, "just normal inquiries," but being escorted to the police station in a police car didn't feel normal at all to Zoe. The officer driving the car either didn't know why the police wanted to talk to her or had been told not to tell her anything. Either way, she got zero information out of him. She leaned back against the seat of the police car and tried to think of another question that would get some details out of the officer.

Her phone rang. It was Jack, of course. He had heard the exchange with the police officer at her hotel door—she'd had her cell phone in her hand at the time.

"I have no idea what's going on," she said, aware that the officer in the driver's seat was listening to every word.

"I'm checking flights." Jack's clipped words and sharp focus told Zoe how worried he was. Unlike Zoe, who became more spontaneous and instinctive under stress, Jack had the opposite reaction. He went straight to logical planning and calculating odds and outcomes.

"But, Jack, the convention. It doesn't end until tomorrow."

"They wouldn't bring you in unless it was crucial to an investigation. That's manpower deployed to locate you. Police forces don't do that on a whim...or even usually for not-so-valuable stolen paintings."

Zoe couldn't argue with that assessment. When they arrived at the police station, she was escorted to a little room with walls the color of wilted celery, but they hadn't taken her cell phone from her, which she thought was a good sign. The cell phone signal wasn't good inside the building, but she sent another text to Jack to let him know she was okay. The little bar that indicated the message was in the process of being sent labored its way across the screen before the phone finally emitted a chime indicating the message had been delivered. At least that would keep Jack up-to-date on what was going on.

The only furnishings in the room were a narrow table of chipped Formica and two folding chairs with plastic seats and backs. The greenish-gray walls were bare except for a square of dark glass on the wall opposite Zoe's chair. Zoe shifted her chair so that she was turned slightly away from the glass. She had that creepy tingling sensation at the back of her neck, indicating that someone was watching her, but she wondered if it was just her imagination.

The door opened, and a man with thinning gray hair and a ruddy, lined face stepped inside and shut the door behind him with precise, efficient movements. He pulled out the chair opposite Zoe and placed a folder on the table between them.

"I'm Inspector Homes." He opened the folder and spoke as he scanned the paper inside the file. "*Homes*, not Holmes. I do not have the letter *l* in my name. No, that is not a joke. Yes, it is my real name." His gaze moved down the paper as he spoke, his voice robotic as if he'd repeated it many times. Then he looked up and studied Zoe. "Now, with that out of the way, tell me about Justine Price."

"Oh, this *is* related to her," Zoe said. "I tried to tell the first officer, but he wasn't interested. Officer Donnelly said he would file a report. He has all the details."

"Officer Donnelly?"

"Yes, he came to Staircase House today and took the information about the break-in and theft."

"Break-in? Theft?"

Zoe's heart, which had ballooned with the hope that this was a routine follow-up inquiry, contracted. "This isn't about the stolen painting, is it?"

Inspector Homes hitched his chair back an inch and folded one leg over the other. "Why don't you tell me about the painting...the stolen painting, and I'll see if it fits." He'd been holding a silver pen in one hand, but he tossed it on the folder and crossed his arms.

"I work for Harrington Throckmorton. I'm a consultant for his firm, Throckmorton Enquiries." Zoe figured throwing out Harrington's name was the best place to begin. She went through everything that had happened since her arrival in Edinburgh.

Homes listened without moving until she finished. "Do you have a business card?" he asked.

Of all the possible questions he could have asked, that one was the last one she expected, but she reached for her messenger bag. "Yes." She extracted one of the thick rectangles with her name and handed it to him.

"This is only your information, not Harrington Throckmorton's."

"Yes," she said. "I'm a consultant. Here, I'll write down his number for you." She used his silver pen to print Harrington's number on the card. "That's his cell phone."

He glanced at it then placed it in the file. "So you met with Justine Price—who you said introduced herself as Poppy Foley—yesterday?"

"Yes."

"And you didn't see her, that is, the woman you now know as Justine, today?"

"No."

"You're sure of that?" He said it mildly, but his gaze darted all over Zoe's face as if he was mentally filing away every flicker of her eyelid or twitch of her mouth.

"I'm sure. I haven't seen her today."

"But you did phone her," he said, and it sounded like an accusation. "Why?"

"To let her know I had the painting," Zoe said, repeating what she'd said earlier.

"Did she return your call?"

"No." Zoe's heartbeat began to thump heavily. "Inspector... Homes," she said, stumbling a bit over his name in her nervousness, "phoning someone isn't a crime. Can you tell me what's going on? Obviously, something has happened that has to do with Justine. What is it?"

"In a moment. To clarify, you phoned her, she didn't call you back, but you went to Staircase House anyway."

"Yes. I was excited to return the painting. I wanted to complete my job. I figured I might catch her at home."

"And that's when you discovered she was an impostor."

"Yes. Officer Donnelly will be able to verify that part of my story."

"Hmm," Homes murmured, and Zoe got the impression that it wasn't that part of her story that he was concerned with.

He put the folder on his crossed leg and made a few notes, then he twisted the pen and flipped the folder closed. "Justine Price is in the hospital. She's unconscious. She was found today at the foot of a set of interior stairs at the Pinnacle Hotel in central Edinburgh. Your phone message to her, stating—and I quote, 'I'm on my way now,' end quote—is the last message on her phone. The doctors tell me her injuries occurred shortly after she received your message."

———

Sergeant Malone, who had observed the conversation between Homes and Mrs. Andrews through the one-way glass, went to his desk and began looking up phone numbers. By the time Homes returned from escorting Mrs. Andrews out of the station, Sergeant Malone had his phone tucked under his chin. He said to Homes, "I'm on hold for Harrington Throckmorton—" He broke off and raised the receiver to his mouth while swiveling his computer monitor toward Homes.

"Yes, that's right," Sergeant Malone said into the phone, "Zoe Andrews...so you confirm it. She *is* working for your company in Edinburgh?"

While Sergeant Malone continued his conversation, Homes scanned the webpage on the computer, the home page of Throckmorton's business.

"Yes, thank you." Malone hung up the phone and turned to Homes. "That was Mr. Throckmorton himself. He confirms Zoe Andrews is here in Edinburgh on assignment for his company, looking for the stolen painting. A Victorian landscape"

"Hmm." Homes had been leaning over the monitor, but now reached for the mouse and clicked to another page.

Sergeant Malone slid his chair to the right, making room for Homes to step closer to the monitor as he clicked through a few more pages of the website. Sergeant Malone didn't say anything else to Homes. Instead, he made a few notes from his phone conversation. He had worked with Homes a long time. There was no rushing him. He would speak when he was ready.

Finally, Homes stood up, his gaze still fixed on the monitor. "No photo," he murmured, "but I think I've met him."

"Throckmorton?" Sergeant Malone asked.

"Yes," Homes said. "The name sounded familiar when the woman mentioned it in the interview." Homes gestured to the monitor. "From the description of the man's history, I think I've met him. If he is who I think he is, he gave a keynote at an international crime prevention conference a few years ago in Geneva. See if you can dig up a photo of him. It may be difficult. He likes to keep a low profile. He made sure all cameras were banned from the lecture hall before he spoke so that his picture wouldn't get out. Understandable, since he often goes undercover to meet with criminals. Wouldn't be smart to do that, if his face was known. If it is the man I remember, then he's legitimate. He's facilitated hundreds of recoveries."

"So maybe the red-headed woman was telling the truth," Sergeant Malone said with a shake of his head. "I thought we would be able to punch a few holes in her story straight away. It's not every day that we get a yarn about stolen paintings and impostors. I quite enjoyed it, actually. Very twisty. It would be even better if *she* was an impostor, too." Sergeant Malone reached for a worn spiral notebook with fragments of paper flaking out of the binder. "Better write down that one." Sergeant Malone planned to write a thriller when he retired in three years.

"One impostor is possible. Two impostors might stretch the believability of the story, I think," Homes said. "All the same, verify her whereabouts today. Perhaps she is an impostor, and she's taking advantage of Justine Price's inability to communicate with us. Perhaps she is the thief, and Justine is the victim." One corner of Homes's mouth quirked down, the only outward sign of his internal thoughts, but Sergeant Malone recognized the tick.

"Don't like the situation?"

"I never like it when I have a possible suspect, but not enough to hold her. Where are we on the interviews from the hotel guests? Have we identified the mystery man spotted outside Price's room?"

"No. Could be that the girl who told us about him just wanted attention. Teenagers are like that. Believe me, I know."

Homes shook his head. "I know you've raised three daughters, and I haven't, but I don't think that was what was going on there. Has the CCTV footage come in?"

"No. Should be here later today."

"Then stay on this Andrews woman. I'm not sure about her yet. Contact Poppy Foley and Officer Donnelly. Follow up on those details then send out an alert with Zoe Andrews' passport details. I want to know if she tries to leave the country."

Zoe settled into the seat of the cab and worked on calming her breathing. Apparently, the police would drive you to their station, but getting back to wherever you were before they interrupted your life was up to you. Zoe wouldn't have accepted a ride in a police car anyway, even if it had been offered. She'd wanted to get out of the dingy mint-toned room as fast as she could. How could they think she'd had something to do with the injuries to Justine?

Was it less than an hour ago that she had been arguing with Jack about how she didn't want to leave Edinburgh until she knew the full story about Justine and the painting? And now she couldn't leave. Inspector Homes's parting words had been, "Please do not leave Edinburgh without getting in touch with me first."

Not exactly the classic, *Don't leave town* line, but close enough to worry her.

At least they hadn't taken her passport.

Justine Price was in the hospital, severely injured. Zoe rubbed her forehead. *Why had she left that message about the painting for Justine? Why hadn't she just called back later?* Realistically, Zoe knew it wouldn't have made any difference. Her call still would have been in the log of Justine's incoming calls. The police would have tracked her down eventually, but Zoe would prefer not to be in the number one position on their go-to suspect list, which is where she was at the moment. Inspector Homes had been polite and mild-mannered, but the way he'd watched her—she shifted in the seat of the cab. She'd felt like he believed she was already guilty and was just waiting for her to admit it. But then again, maybe that was his approach with all his interviews.

Zoe's phone rang. It was Jack. "Zoe, where are you? I called, but your phone just went to voicemail."

"I'm fine. I'm on my way back to the hotel." She caught him up on what had happened. "So I can't leave now, at least not until they figure out I didn't hurt Justine."

"That probably won't take them long," Jack said. "What time did it happen...the attack on Justine?"

"I don't know, exactly. It must have been close to eleven-thirty because my call was the last one she received, and they were pretty interested in that. The inspector didn't give away much information, but he seemed to think that I called her and went directly to see her when she didn't answer."

"Which is what happened, but you went to Staircase

House. Since Justine wasn't there, and one of the people who *was* there was a police officer, I think you'll be okay."

"Right," Zoe said. "I know that, but I don't like the whole situation. I hate that I'm mixed up in this. And I certainly didn't want Harrington to have to vouch for me to the police on my first job for him."

"Zoe, it's not your fault that Justine lied to you."

"But I shouldn't have taken her at her word."

"Harrington did."

"Okay, that does make me feel marginally better."

"It should. Harrington can't blame you for doing the same thing he did. And if he does, then he's not the sort of person you want to work for."

"You're right," Zoe said. She knew his words were true, but inside, she still felt like a failure.

"Have you talked to Harrington?" Jack asked.

"Briefly. Just a few minutes ago. He says the police have already contacted him to confirm my story. He was extremely nice, said I wasn't to worry about anything, that it would be fine. He seemed to think it wasn't that big of a deal."

"He works with the police all the time."

"Right, but working with them and being questioned by them are two different things. At least he wasn't upset."

"Harrington strikes me as the type of person who has a long fuse. It would take more than you being questioned by the police to get him worked up. On another subject, I'm on the flight that arrives tomorrow at nine."

"That's good," Zoe said, knowing that their budget would take the hit for a last-minute trans-Atlantic airfare, but she would be glad when Jack arrived. "Maybe by then I'll be in the clear about the attack on Justine, and we can concentrate on figuring out what's going on with the painting."

"One thing at a time," Jack said. "I'll see you tomorrow."

"Sounds good. And, Jack, thanks for not saying you told me so."

A small laugh came over the line. "What do you think I am, a novice husband? I've been doing this for going on three years now. I know that being married means never saying I told you so."

Zoe hung up and realized she was actually smiling. After the day she'd had, that was pretty amazing. Jack had that effect on her—being with him, just talking on the phone with him, somehow seemed to smooth the bumps in life.

The taxi had been making its way slowly through the streets toward her hotel while she'd been on the phone. She had barely noticed the surroundings, but as the driver made a turn, a sign caught Zoe's eye, The Pinnacle Hotel.

She leaned forward. "Excuse me, was that the Pinnacle Hotel in the city center?"

"Yes, ma'am."

"I'll get out here."

## 9

INSPECTOR HOMES HADN'T GIVEN UP much info about the attack on Justine, but Zoe knew one thing about it—the location. The sliding glass doors of the Pinnacle Hotel swished open as she neared them. She walked into the noisy lobby filled with groups of people clustered around piles of suitcases. The cheap furnishings and barely existent decorating scheme reminded Zoe of budget hotels in the States. She figured this was the European equivalent of a super discounted hotel chain.

Zoe wasn't quite sure what she hoped to accomplish. She was acting more on instinct, which was how she liked to roll, so when she surveyed the lobby and spotted a uniformed police officer waiting for an elevator, she headed in that direction. Two other people stepped into the elevator with her and the police officer. Zoe waited until the police officer punched the button for the fourth floor then she said, "Six, please." He pushed it for her and gave everyone a nod as he stepped out on the fourth floor.

When the elevator reached the sixth floor, Zoe waved the couple out of the elevator in front of her and trailed along behind them, digging in her messenger bag as if she were searching for a keycard until they disappeared into a room. Once they were out of sight, Zoe strode along the corridor. It bent in an L-shape, and she found a door marked STAIRS at the end of the shorter leg of the corridor.

Zoe tried the handle. It turned easily and silently. She pulled the door open a few inches. The landing was empty. She poked her head in and listened. Below, a door clanged, and voices floated up from a landing several floors down.

"All right, that's the last of the evidence techs. I'll tell the manager we're done here. He'll have to get someone in here to clean. You get the tape."

"We're not leaving the tape up?" a voice asked in reply.

"Can't. It's the fire escape route, the only one for this side of the building. It has to be open."

"Right," said the first man. "I'll meet you in the lobby." Zoe heard what sounded like paper or plastic crumpling.

The crumpling sound went on for a few seconds, accompanied by a few heavy footfalls, then the door thudded closed, its echo booming up and down the concrete of the stairs. With a last glance over her shoulder to make sure no one was behind her, Zoe slipped through the door and closed it quietly behind her. She tiptoed down the stairs to a landing at the halfway point between floors where the stairs folded back on themselves. She looked over the railing and saw a dark pool that made her swallow hard. The last few stairs and a lower portion of the wall were smeared with streaks of dried blood.

Zoe crept down a few steps and looked around. Black powder covered the handrail and the door. Zoe tucked her hands in her pockets. They wouldn't find a record of her fingerprints here, a point in her favor. The only other things on the staircase that Zoe could see were dust and a few blobs of dried gum. The crime scene technicians had probably bagged any stray bits of paper, gum wrappers, or frayed threads that had been on the stairs. She checked the sign by the door—this was the fourth floor—then scurried back up to the fifth floor. She looked out the window and saw an officer moving away from her down the hallway. He'd come from a room where the door was propped open. A flash of light from inside the room brightened the hallway for a second. Two more rapid bursts of light followed. The crime scene technicians must have moved on to what had been Justine's room.

Zoe retraced her steps to the landing of the sixth floor then took the elevator down again. She would have liked a glimpse at Justine's hotel room, but she wasn't foolish enough to try to accomplish that with police officers moving around the hotel. The lobby area was still packed with people. Zoe worked through the crowd and settled onto a thinly padded couch then smiled at a woman seated on the other end. "So crowded."

The woman rolled her eyes. "We've been here three days, and it's always like this. Every day it's a new tour bus arriving."

"What is going on with the police?" Zoe said, raising her chin in the direction of an officer slipping out a side exit.

The woman twisted around. "The police? I have no idea. Frank, did you see that, the police are here."

Frank hadn't seen and wasn't interested. After a few moments of chitchat about Edinburgh's sites, Zoe moved on to the next group. She'd worked her way through three clusters of tourists, striking up what she hoped people took as a casual conversation as they waited for a harried tour guide to distribute keycards. Finally, a petite teen with heavily made-up eyes looked up from her cell phone after her mother heard the name "Summerby" called and hurried off to get their keys. The girl dipped a shoulder and flicked her long brown hair over her shoulder as she looked toward Zoe. "You want to know what the police are doing here?" she asked in an American accent.

Under all the make-up, Zoe could see that she was young, probably thirteen or fourteen. "Yes."

"A woman was pushed down the stairs," she said with a relish that brought back memories of high school, where drama was practically a currency. "She was in the room next to ours. That's why we're down here." The girl sighed. "Mom insisted on moving. Says we can't stay on that floor. It's too dangerous."

"Well, if a woman was hurt..." Zoe said.

"It wasn't some random thing. They knew each other."

"They?"

"The woman and the guy who pounded on her door."

"You saw him?"

"Yeah. I was on my way back from looking for an ice machine. Did you know they don't have them here? Weird, huh? Anyway, he was banging on her door. She yelled through the door and told him to go away, but he didn't."

"What happened?"

"I don't know. I went in our room. She let him in, I think, because I could still hear them, but the sounds were different, closer."

"Could you hear what they said?" Zoe asked with a quick glance over her shoulder. There must be some problem because the mom wasn't on her way back. She was arguing with a hotel employee.

"Nah, just that he was mad. At first, it was him yelling, then she got louder. Finally, the door slammed. I figured he'd left, but then a few seconds later, I heard screaming and went to see what was going on. It was a maid—a whole floor below us," the teen said, visibly impressed at the maid's carrying voice. "I couldn't see anything, and of course, my mom dragged me away as soon as she could. I didn't know it was the lady next to us until the police came and talked to us."

"So they know all this? You told them?"

"Sure," she said, giving a one-shouldered shrug.

The mom returned, flushed, but clutching a small envelope with keycards. "Come on, Haley. Our new rooms are finally ready."

"See you," Haley said, popping her earbuds in and grabbing a suitcase handle to follow her mom.

"Wait, Haley," Zoe said, hurrying after the teen.

Haley's mom had paused to talk to another woman, a conversation that involved lots of hand gestures and head nods. She didn't notice Zoe approach her daughter. Haley took out an earbud. "Yeah?"

"This is important. What did the guy look like?"

"Umm, I mostly saw his back, but he glanced at me as I walked by. He was kind of old, but not *really* old...probably about my mom's age."

Zoe ran a quick glance over Haley's mom and guessed she was somewhere in her mid-thirties. "Anything else?" Zoe asked, turning back to Haley.

"I suppose you'd call his hair red, but it was kind of orange. It was the first thing I noticed about him. It wasn't long exactly, but it was shaggy... kind of all over the place. And he was tall."

Considering her petite stature, Zoe thought that most people were probably taller than Haley, but she kept that thought to herself. "Anything else? What was he wearing?"

"A long coat. It was dark, too. Black or brown or something like that. And he had a scarf," she added suddenly. "I'd forgotten about that, but as I walked by, he was tucking it into the collar of his coat. He had on gloves. Leather ones."

A pulse of excitement ran through Zoe. "Okay. That's great. You're sure about the scarf?" It might not mean anything, Zoe thought, but the description was similar to the description of the guy who sold the painting to Nancy's daughter.

"What did the scarf look like?" Zoe asked. Nancy had been specific about the scarf.

"I don't remember."

"Not even a color?" Zoe asked, not wanting to mention any specific color or pattern—like plaid—that might influence Haley's memory.

"I don't know," Haley said with a shrug.

"But you're sure he had a scarf?"

"Yes." The girl's chin tilted up. "I know what I saw."

A tall man wearing an overcoat and scarf matched Nancy's description of the man who sold the painting. On the other hand, it could be two completely different men. There were probably tons of tall, thirtyish men wearing a coat and a scarf in Edinburgh. "I'm not doubting you. I just wanted to make sure. It's important. Did you tell all this to the police?"

"Yeah, except the part about the scarf."

"You or your mom should call them back and tell them about it."

"Oh, I can do that. I'll send that inspector-guy a text. He gave me his card." She extracted a business card from the pocket of her skintight jeans then her fingers flew across the tiny keyboard of her phone.

"Anything else you remember?"

Haley paused and fixed her black-rimmed eyes on Zoe. "You sure are curious."

"I think that guy you saw may be involved in a...business transaction that I was part of." Zoe hoped that sounded important enough to justify her nosiness but vague enough not to give away anything important.

Haley raised her eyebrows. "Okay." She drew out the last syllable as she raised her eyebrows, but she went back to her text.

"Thanks for talking to me, Haley. You've been helpful."

"Sure. Whatever. Beats standing around here, waiting...or being dragged through another castle."

"Can I give you my number, in case you think of anything else?"

"Yeah, I guess so," Haley said as she finished her text and fingered her earbud.

They exchanged numbers. Haley's mom seemed to be wrapping up her conversation, so Zoe thanked Haley again and was about to turn away, when Haley said, "Oh yeah. Since you're so interested, I guess you'd want to know that when she yelled at the guy, she called him Theo."

## 10

"BUT I THOUGHT YOU SAID you couldn't understand what they were saying," Zoe said to Haley.

"Well, yeah, once I went inside our room it was all garbled and just noise, but before, when I was in the hall, she yelled, 'Go away, Theo.' *That* was as clear as when my mom yells at me from the kitchen to come down for dinner."

When Zoe emerged from the hotel a few minutes later, she spotted a sign pointing to the Royal Mile. It was only a few blocks away, so she decided to walk. The haze of disbelief and shock at being questioned by the police had worn off, and with the tidbits of information she had now, she felt rejuvenated. She wasn't about to rely on the police to clear her of any involvement in Justine's injuries. Sitting back and waiting for things to work out was never a good plan in her book. Things went better when she was proactive. She'd call in a few favors and see what she could find out on her own. As she strode along in the bracing cold air, she found Carla's number.

A groggy voice answered. "What?"

"Carla, I'm sorry. I completely forgot about the time change." Like Zoe, Carla hated early starts. She often worked late into the night then slept the morning away. She said she did her best work after nine at night.

"Zoe?"

"Yes. It's me. I'm sorry. I'll call back later. I'm in Edinburgh, and I'm so flustered that I didn't think about the time change."

"Edinburgh. Cool." Carla sounded a bit more coherent. "What are you doing there?"

"I was supposed to be recovering a painting, but things have gotten a bit complicated. But don't worry about it. Go back to sleep. I'll call you later."

"It's no use now. I'm awake. I'll just go to bed early tonight to make up for it—I'll turn in at two a.m., instead of three. Let me get the coffee going." Carla's voice changed as she moved. "There, I'm up, and the coffee is brewing. No going back now. Besides, your life is always interesting...much more interesting than mine, which is unfair. I'm the hacker, after all."

"I thought you were a reformed hacker."

"Yeah, yeah. Details. I have to keep my hand in," Carla said. "Stay current. I wear a white hat now. Mostly. So what's up? What's complicated?"

"Ah, something that might require a hat of a different color."

"Better and better. Is the painting still missing?"

"No. It's been returned," Zoe said.

"But isn't that problem solved?" Carla actually sounded disappointed.

"No. I've just been interviewed by the police."

"Oh, this was so worth waking up for."

Zoe summarized what had happened since she arrived in Edinburgh. By the time she finished, Carla was noisily sipping coffee and asking questions. "So you think this Theo guy is the same person who sold the painting to the art dealer?"

"Possibly."

"And if he sold it, then he probably stole it."

"Again, possibly."

"When did you get so cautious and thoughtful?" Carla said.

"Chatting with the police makes you that way."

"I suppose so. Okay, so you probably want me to see if I can find a link between the woman who was hurt and this Theo guy."

"Do you think that's possible?"

"Yes, my dear, I'm not as wishy-washy as you. I'm sure I can find something. Give me all the info you've got on them."

"It's not much. Her name is Justine Price. She's a nurse. She went to school with Poppy Foley, but I don't know the name of the school. She worked for Poppy's family, nursing Poppy's father. I'm not sure what his name was. He recently died."

"Excellent."

Zoe wasn't sure she'd heard Carla's words correctly. "Excellent?"

"Records, Zoe. Public records are a gold mine of information."

"Oh. See, that's why I called you." Zoe continued, "Let's see, what else? Poppy's family owns Staircase House in Edinburgh and an estate in Devon. Frampton Downs, I think it was called."

"More public records. You're making this too easy for me."

"Okay, I'll stop. That's all I've got anyway, except for the guy's first name. Theo."

"Don't worry about that. If there's a link between Justine and Theo, I'll find it. What about this painting you were hired to find?"

"It's called *A View of Edinburgh*. One of the Foley ancestors painted it, Annabel Foley. She's famous for her botanicals, but this is a landscape, one of her early works. But that's not the main issue right now."

"Right. I'll concentrate on Justine and Theo, but I'll nose around a bit and check out the painting. It's always good to have all the information you can get."

"Yes." Zoe was about to thank her and hang up, but instead she said, "Carla, don't do anything that you feel uncomfortable with." Zoe was fine with pushing the boundaries herself, but she didn't want to be the one to push Carla out of her comfort zone.

Carla made a raspberry noise. "This will be easy peasy, as my niece says."

"You won't have to go back to the dark side?"

"No, only the gray zone. I'll call you back soon."

When she hung up, Zoe realized she was starving and made a detour into the next restaurant she came to, a Thai place with a buffet. Zoe loaded up her plate and thought about her next move as she ate. Carla's words about how it was good to have all the information possible came back to her. Jack said that, too, and it was something she'd learned the hard way over the last few years. A gap in knowledge could lead to a huge mess in the future.

She pressed her napkin to her lips and dialed another phone number. She hadn't heard back from Henri Masard, which wasn't surprising. She and Jack had been in touch with him a few times since their adventure in Paris, and each time he'd been lackadaisical about returning their calls.

This time, he answered her call, all but singing her name in his French-accented English. "Zoe Andrews, how are you?" He didn't wait for her to answer, but went on. "I was so happy to hear your message. I am traveling and everything is up in the air, as you would say, so I was not able to call you back. What can I help you with? You mentioned a painting by Annabel Foley?"

"Yes. I'm working with Harrington Throckmorton."

"Yes, of course. Very good at what he does. I heard he has created his own enterprise. "

"Yes. I hope you can help us. We were hired to find an Annabel Foley landscape."

"Not a botanical?"

"No. One of her early pieces, *A View of Edinburgh*."

"Why would someone steal one of her landscapes? They are not valuable at all, in comparison to her later works."

"That's exactly my question. Two of her botanical paintings were on either side of the landscape that was stolen. I'm not an expert, but they were beautiful. Even I could tell they were special."

"Curious. And the painting is still missing?"

"No, it has been found, but other things have happened that make me wonder if it's more valuable than we realize." Zoe went on to describe the attack on Justine and the police's involvement.

A few seconds of silence filled the line. Then Masard said, "It puzzles me. I would like to see the painting. Would that be possible?"

"No, I returned it to the owner, but despite that, she's not happy with me."

"Well, without seeing it, I cannot tell you much," he said, and Zoe could picture his Gallic shrug that would accompany the statement. "And even then, to be complete in your investigation, you would need certain tests...infrared reflectography and other scans. X-rays...things of that nature. There could be any number of reasons that painting might be more valuable than anyone realizes. My first thought is that it might be a recycled canvas. If Foley painted over another work—perhaps not her own since it is from early in her career—then it could be valuable. I cannot remember, did she move in any artistic circles with other famous painters?"

"I don't know," Zoe said, making notes on her paper napkin. "But if there was a valuable painting under the Foley landscape, how would anyone know about it? And if it's there, why would the thief sell it to a dealer?"

Masard said, "All astute questions. Of course, it could be that the value is not in the painting itself."

"You mean in the frame? Something might be hidden in it?"

"It is possible. I do not see why someone would take a

Foley landscape when they had the choice of two of her botanicals."

"They were gorgeous paintings, Henri. I only had time to glance at them, but the colors were vivid and the artwork was so detailed. I wanted to look at them longer."

"And you saw the landscape painting when you returned it?"

"Yes," Zoe said, kicking herself for not examining it more closely. "I had a local dealer verify it for me. She seems knowledgeable about Foley's paintings, and Harrington trusts her."

"Well, that is an impeccable recommendation, if Harrington trusts her. She didn't notice anything unusual about the painting?"

"No, but she was specifically looking at it to make sure it was the Foley landscape. I wish I'd looked more closely at the frame or even the back of the painting."

"You did not look at the back?" Masard said in tones of astonishment.

"No," Zoe said, miserably. "I should have. I should have remembered." During their previous adventure with Masard, the back of a painting had proved to be as critical as the front.

"Ah, well. Do not be too hard on yourself," Masard said. "You will not forget now."

"Doesn't do me a lot of good now, though."

"You could not ask to see it again?"

Zoe blew out a breath. "Yes, I could ask."

Poppy could only say no.

Sergeant Malone moved the video forward another few seconds, made a note, then repeated the process. He'd been doing it for hours.

"How is it going?" A voice asked from over his shoulder.

Sergeant Malone spun his chair away from the monitor to speak to Homes. "Same. Nothing, except the ginger-haired bloke outside her hotel door."

"Nothing interesting from the lobby cameras?" Homes asked. He stood as he always did when thinking, the elbow of one arm propped on the other arm, which was folded across his chest. His chin rested on the fingers of his bent arm—sort of a standing version of Rodin's *The Thinker*.

"Nothing but a headache." Sergeant Malone waved to his notepad, which was covered with printed notes. "Tour bus unloaded around the time we estimate the attack took place, but I haven't seen our ginger fellow, so I don't think he was with the tour. I'm almost through all of the footage. I don't think he's going to show up."

"Perhaps he came in the side entrance that isn't covered by the cameras. Can you bring up the footage from the hallway? I haven't seen it yet."

Sergeant Malone clicked a few keys and the image changed to a hallway lined with doors on either side. "I'll get it to the relevant bit." He fast-forwarded until a tall man with a broad-shouldered build in an overcoat and scarf exited the elevator. The color on the recording wasn't strong, but his reddish hair was clear enough to add it to the list of identifying characteristics, which also included a height of at least two meters. Only his back was visible, but his walk spoke volumes. He was agitated. He marched down the corridor and hammered on the Price woman's door. The video didn't record sound, so they had no idea what he said.

As they watched the video, Sergeant Malone said, "I ran her cell phone records. Normal stuff, take-out services, a relative in Derbyshire—an aunt. But she did make several calls within the last few weeks to a Theodore Cooke." Sergeant Malone froze the video and opened a new window on his computer. "This is his current driving license."

"Looks like the same man," Homes said, his gaze bouncing back and forth between the two images on the screen. "Similar hair color and height. What's his connection to Justine Price?"

"Can't find one. Not yet, anyway. Doesn't live near her. She has a flat in London. He lives in Manchester. She's a nurse. He's...well, he seems to prefer to make his living in less legitimate ways. A couple of convictions—burglary. Homes, no cars. Nothing high-end."

"Let's locate him."

Sergeant Malone nodded and set the video in motion again. "There's the young girl. Video confirms her version." On the video, a teen with long dark hair came down the hallway from the elevator, her attention focused on her phone until the man raised his arm and pounded on the door, which drew an immediate reaction from her. She looked up, increased her pace, and skirted around him before slipping into the room next door to the door he was repeatedly hitting. After a few seconds, the door in front of the man opened an inch, and he shoved inside.

Homes shook his head. "Why did she open the door? All

she had to do was call the front desk. They would have him removed."

Sergeant Malone didn't answer the rhetorical question. It was one of the hardest parts of the job—looking at things after the fact and seeing how one small decision turned a person's life upside down. He sighed and fast-forwarded. "Less than a minute later."

The door opened. A woman emerged, her eyes wide with fright as she looked toward the elevator momentarily. She must have decided she didn't want to wait for the elevator. She sprinted for the stairs. *Another of those split-second decisions*, Sergeant Malone thought. One that almost cost the woman her life.

The man in the overcoat raced out of the room after her. Only a few steps behind, he reached the stairwell door seconds after the woman. "That's it." Sergeant Malone hit a key and the monitor went back to the lobby recording. "No cameras on the stairs."

"And no record of the man leaving?" Homes asked.

"No. He must have slipped out the same way he came in. The side door, I bet, like you said."

"And what about the red-headed American woman, Zoe Andrews?"

"Not a trace. If she was in a disguise—say a wig or something like that—it's possible that she could have come in with the tour group, but she did not arrive looking like we saw her."

Homes massaged his chin. "And you haven't seen her on the fourth floor video?"

"No. And she didn't show up on any of the other video

from the other floors either." Homes chuckled, and Sergeant Malone said, "I knew you'd ask. I think she's clear."

Homes shifted to sit on the edge of a near-by desk, but kept his chin cradled in his hand. "Then that would mean she was telling us the truth."

"Apparently so." Sergeant Malone's gaze shifted to his notebook of ideas. He'd have to write this one up. Good fodder for his future book.

"Her story checks out," Homes continued, thinking aloud. "She wasn't near Justine Price at the time of the attack, and her employer confirmed her assignment in Edinburgh was to recover the painting, which Poppy Foley says she did return. So we have two separate people—Justine Price and Zoe Hunter—connected to the Victorian painting, which isn't worth that much."

Sergeant Malone raised his eyebrows.

"Yes," Homes said. "I checked it out with a few experts. Worth a few hundred euro on the open market. Nothing extravagant."

"Odd."

Homes was silent a moment, then said, "Any connection between the American woman and this Theodore Cooke?"

"Haven't checked." Sergeant Malone made a note. "But I will."

Homes's phone buzzed. He removed it from his pocket and read a text. "I'll be at the hospital, if you need me. Justine Price is awake."

_____

## 11

ZOE PRESSED THE MODERN DOORBELL outside
Staircase House for the second time that day and braced
for a confrontation. She hoped that by going to Staircase
House in person, rather than calling Poppy, it would make it
harder for Poppy to say no. Zoe put the odds at about a seventy
percent chance that Poppy would close the door in her face.
She didn't seem to be a person who was easily swayed.

After a few seconds, the iron-studded door swung open,
and Poppy said, "Oh, good. I was going to call you."

"You were?" Zoe glanced around uncertainly, unsure how
to handle the offhanded greeting. She'd expected ranting or a
quick door slam.

"Yes," Poppy said. "Come in, please. I have something I'd
like to discuss with you."

Zoe followed her up the curving staircase to the high-
ceiling room. Poppy gestured to the seats in front of the over-
sized fireplace, and Zoe settled onto a cushion, amazed that

Poppy had invited her inside. Only a few hours earlier, Poppy had been accusing her of being a thief.

Poppy sat down in a chair across from Zoe. The painting was still on the end table, but the brown wrapping paper had been removed. Zoe had taken a seat as close to the painting as she could get. She scanned the painting, trying to memorize every detail, from the frame to the brushstrokes.

"My brother just rang me, which is a bit unusual. We're not extremely close. He nattered on about several inconsequential things, but finally got around to what he really wanted—information about this." She raised her eyebrows and shifted her gaze toward the painting. "He has never shown any interest in art or paintings. Something is going on. I want you to find out why he called me out of the blue to ask about *A View of Edinburgh*. What is so special about this painting?"

"Yes, of course, I can look into that," Zoe said, even though she wasn't exactly sure how she'd go about it. Harrington had said she had latitude to work on her own. He might not have been thinking of quite this much latitude, but she couldn't pass up this opportunity. She'd figure out a way to make it work for her and for Poppy. The important thing was that it would give her access to the painting. And Poppy was a family friend of Harrington's, another reason to say yes and try to keep her happy. Although, Poppy seemed like the sort of person who lived most of her life in a moody, dissatisfied state. Perhaps "not angry" was a better way to describe the emotional state Zoe hoped to achieve with Poppy. "Perhaps he heard about the theft?" Zoe said.

"I'm sure Robbie heard about it. He didn't ask directly, but I know my brother. He tiptoed around the subject and was careful not to mention it, which means he knew. He could never keep secrets from me. He's transparent, at least to me. What I want to know is how did he find out, and why does he care? He wouldn't waste a minute of his time on it, if there wasn't some angle for him."

"May I?" Zoe asked, reaching for the painting.

"Yes."

Zoe picked it up carefully, mentally telling herself to go slow and examine each part of it. She'd already looked at the brushstrokes and the painting itself with Violet, but she studied the scene again. No amazing revelation popped out at her. Next, she carefully looked at each section of the thick wooden frame. It was solidly constructed. No cracks or fissures marred the surface, except for the scratch that was also visible in the photograph that Justine had given her. Zoe ran her fingers over the scratch, but the wood didn't give or shift under the pressure of her fingers. Zoe turned her attention to the back of the painting. Yellowed with age, the only mark was a peeling sticker in the bottom left-hand corner with a zero followed by a seven.

"What is that?" Poppy had shifted around and was standing behind Zoe's chair, peering over her shoulder.

"A cataloging mark, I think. Do you have an inventory of your family's paintings? Or of Annabel Foley's?"

Poppy frowned as she strode over to a set of bookshelves. "I do remember someone mentioning an inventory...perhaps a solicitor? Yes, I think that was it. He recommended an update as the last one was done years and years ago. Positively ancient, he said. Probably by Aunt Aggie. She had that Victorian cataloging and classification bug. She wrote down everything." Poppy ran her finger along the shelves. "Yes, here they are. The Agatha Foley section. She was Annabel's sister. Annabel was the visual one, the painter. Aggie was into words. They were quite a pair. Very liberated for their time. Traveled the world together—without a chaperone, which was quite shocking in those days—after their father died. If anyone catalogued Annabel's paintings it would be Aggie."

Zoe kept in contact with her immediate relatives, but she knew little about any of her relatives beyond her grandparents' generation. What would it be like to know what your ancestors did during their lifetime and to call them by nicknames? It was a strange concept to Zoe, who tended to keep her distance from her relatives. Being let down by the people closest to her had made her skittish, but there was a warmth in Poppy's tone as she talked about Annabel and Aggie that Zoe hadn't heard before.

Zoe carefully turned the painting back over and put it down face up on the table then joined Poppy at the bookshelves. Poppy pulled out several dusty books. "Here, have a look at these." She handed a stack of books to Zoe then motioned her to a table at the back of the room near a floor-to-ceiling window.

Zoe placed the books on the table. Some were hardback books with rich gold lettering on the spines and beautiful swirled patterns on the endpapers. Two of the books were softbound, the pages and covers flexing under Zoe's fingers. Strings tied in a knot held the loose leather cover around one of the softbound books. The books looked intriguing, but her thoughts were still with the painting.

"Earlier, you mentioned a family legend about a treasure. Could that have something to do with the painting?"

Poppy shifted her head, shaking her hair away from her face as she looked up at the ceiling. "My father thought it did, but as I told you, he wasn't exactly thinking straight near the end, if you know what I mean."

"Perhaps you'd better tell me about the legend anyway. It may not be true, but if someone thinks it is...then that could account for the sudden interest in the painting."

Poppy gripped the back of one of the chairs. "It's just a silly rhyme. It can't seriously mean anything."

"What is it?" When Zoe arrived, Poppy hadn't offered to take her coat or bag, so Zoe still had her messenger bag slung across her chest. She dug inside and found her notebook.

Poppy raised her eyebrows. "Fine. 'The rosy-fingered vista of the empress will guide you to the sister.'"

Zoe scribbled it down then looked up, perplexed. "I don't get it."

"No one does. It doesn't make sense. It was fun to imagine it meant something when we were kids, but it doesn't mean anything."

Zoe glanced at the stack of books. "It does mention a sister."

Poppy flicked her hand. "Of course, that's what Robbie and I latched on to when we were kids, but we hunted all over Frampton and here, too. Nothing related to the sisters at all."

"But you said they were great travelers. Were they the ones who supposedly brought back something valuable?"

Poppy pulled back a chair wearily and gestured for Zoe to have a seat at the table. "I'll give you the whole story," she said in a resigned tone. "Aggie and Annabel did travel, and they brought back all sorts of things...paintings, books, statues, scraps of parchment, jewelry. They were quite big on relics. They brought back lots of scraps of papyrus from Egypt—copies of the New Testament—they were thrilled with them. They were both deeply religious. It was the era, you know. But they donated all of that—the papyrus—to the university." Poppy ran her hand along the grain of the wood table. "Robbie's friend Ivan, who is rather a book fiend, looked into it. When they were kids, he and Robbie used the legend as an excuse to creep into every dusty corner they could find. They also dug up the front lawn at Frampton one holiday when they were home from school. Father was incensed and put a stop to all their treasure hunting. But I do know that Ivan checked later about the papyrus, because he's bookish and into that sort of thing, but there was nothing to it."

"What happened to Aggie and Annabel? Did they talk about a treasure? Is that how the legend started?" Zoe glanced at the stack of books with renewed interest.

"No, the word 'treasure' is never mentioned." Poppy touched the corner of one of the books. "I've read Aggie's travelogues and her diary." Poppy's eyebrows pressed together creating a tiny wrinkle between them. "They both died in the winter of 1895, within a few weeks of each other. Influenza. Aggie mentioned the rhyme in her diary that year. They were getting a bit weaker and weren't traveling as much. They had stayed in England, and Aggie was cataloging all of Annabel's paintings." She gestured to one of the softbound leather books. "Aggie became ill first. She liked puzzles and puns and cyphers. I think Annabel made up the rhyme to entertain her sister."

Zoe looked up from her notebook. "You sound as if they were friends of yours."

She shrugged. "Big lonely house. Lots of time on my hands when I was a kid. I read."

"What happened after they died? Did they have children?"

"No. Never married. The estate went to a nephew, Fredrick. He was awful. The aunts said he was a wastrel, and they were quite right. He ran the estate into the ground. Fortunately he didn't live long enough to completely destroy everything. My grandfather inherited the estate when Fred had one too many and fell out the window of a brothel."

"Wow."

Poppy nodded. "A real winner, I know."

Zoe looked at her notes. "So Fredrick...any mention of the treasure associated with him?"

"He wasn't quite as good a record keeper as Aggie, but he did have all the walls ripped out at Frampton—that's another family story. Went quite potty about it, apparently. Insisted that the treasure was there and that the aunts had hidden it from him since they disliked him." Poppy's gaze shifted to the high ceilinged room. "Thank goodness he never came here. He hated the north. I'd dread to see what he would have done to this place. We probably wouldn't have any paneling at all."

Poppy scooted her chair back. "That's enough about my family history. I'm sure you're completely bored."

"No. It's fascinating stuff." Zoe closed her notebook. "If you want to know absolutely everything about the painting, then there are some tests that should be run on it," Zoe said.

"Do it. You can arrange that?" Poppy asked as she stood.

"Yes. I know an art dealer who could take a look at it as well."

"Set it up." Poppy retrieved the painting and put it on the table beside the books.

"The person I have in mind lives in Paris," Zoe said. "It may take a few days to coordinate travel for him to come here."

"Then see if you can take it to him," Poppy said. "I'll cover the travel costs, of course. You're surprised," she said, studying Zoe's face.

"Well, it's just that earlier today you wanted me out of here. You said it was a family matter and were clearly anxious to end any questions about the painting." *And there was also the little accusation of me being a thief*, Zoe thought.

"Yes, I have made a complete turnaround, haven't I?" Poppy ran her hand along the back of one of the chairs. "Before, I thought it was only Justine involved." She rolled her eyes. "Justine is rather slippery. I was so desperate to get someone to care for Father, someone who wouldn't upset him, that I turned a blind eye to her personality. I realize now that I shouldn't have done that. Foolish on my part, but now that Robbie is interested in the painting..." Her words trailed off as she drew the painting to her and looked at it. "Robbie is a good kid, but he's frighteningly optimistic and has a tendency to be drawn to every possible scheme to make money. He actually fell into one that made money, a price comparison mobile app, but I'm afraid that the money he made from that thing is long gone. I'm sure he's shifted it into other 'opportunities.' With him, it is like tossing money into the wind. I've tried to talk to him about long-term investments, but he laughs and says why accept a return of a few percent when the return could be over one-hundred percent?" She shook her head. "He doesn't ever seem to remember that the one-hundred percent return is like a lightning strike—possible, but extremely rare and almost impossible to predict." She returned the painting to the varnished surface of the table. "The police have found Justine. She was attacked and is in the hospital. Did you know that?"

"Yes," Zoe said simply, not wanting to mention that the police had requested her presence to discuss it.

Poppy went on, "I'm sure Robbie had nothing to do with that—he isn't violent. Just the opposite, in fact. So charming and considerate that he made my friends' match-making mothers drool. But while he's sweet, I'm afraid he may have been drawn into something...dangerous, maybe even thuggish. I need to find out why he's suddenly interested in *A View of Edinburgh*, and if it is connected in any way to Justine."

Zoe decided to keep the information that Carla was digging into about Theo to herself for the moment. She wanted to know more before she shared those details with Poppy.

"How soon can you start?" Poppy asked.

"I'll make some calls today and let you know about the tests."

"Do you need a retainer?" Poppy asked.

"No, I'm sure Harrington wouldn't want to do that since you're a family friend, and there was a—ah, misunderstanding earlier. What I will need to do is send you a statement of work. It will detail exactly what I'll do. I'll need you to sign it, then I'll return and pick up the painting."

"Let's do it now." Poppy went to a desk and opened a drawer. She returned to the table with a legal pad. "I'm not worried you'll steal the painting, if that's what you're concerned about. You've already returned it once. I think I can trust you with it."

Zoe reached for the paper. "Thank you for trusting me, I do appreciate it. But I will need the agreement signed. In case there are any questions."

"And you'll report back to me the moment you find anything." It was a statement, not a question.

## 12

ZOE LEFT STAIRCASE HOUSE WITH the painting wrapped in a fresh layer of brown paper, the original statement of work with Poppy's signature, and the old books from the Foley library. She called Harrington. He answered as she stepped out of the tunnel-like passageway to the Royal Mile. "I have some good news. Poppy wants me to research the painting."

"She wants to know what all the fuss is about, does she?" Harrington said. "I can't say I'm surprised. You accepted the job?"

"Yes. I know I should have contacted you before—"

"No," Harrington interrupted her, "you did exactly the right thing. Poppy is not someone who likes to be kept waiting. If you'd put her off while you checked with me, she likely would have contacted someone else. If we can close the loop on this painting, find some answers, it will be to the benefit of both Poppy and us."

Zoe let out a breath she'd been holding. "Okay, good. I'm glad you see it that way, too." Harrington said he would send her a list of tests that she could check against those that Masard would recommend then signed off.

Zoe went straight to the hotel and popped the painting in the safe in her room. It fit with millimeters to spare. As she closed the safe, her phone chimed with a text.

It was from Jack. *On flight. See you in the a.m.*

Zoe dropped down on the bed as she tapped out a reply. *So much to tell you when you get here. A lot has happened.*

*Good or bad?* He texted back immediately.

*Mostly good.* Getting rehired to uncover the truth about the painting was a good thing in Zoe's book. *Don't worry. Not under arrest or anything.*

*Glad to hear it.* Jack finished off his message with one of those happy-faced emoticons, which made Zoe smile. Who would have thought that her straight-laced, all-business husband would send emoticons? This one was a happy face blowing a kiss. He sent one more message. *Closing door now. Have to go. See you soon.*

Zoe settled back against the headboard and dialed Masard's number. He answered in French, but switched to English as soon as Zoe identified herself.

"Henri, I have the painting."

"I knew you could convince her to see it again—" he broke off abruptly. Then he said, "No, I won't ask you how you obtained it."

"In a perfectly honest way. The woman who owns it has hired me to find out why it is suddenly so popular. I'd like you to take a look at it. I can bring it to you. Would you be able to look at it tomorrow?"

"No, I cannot. I am not in Paris. At the moment, I am in Salzburg."

Zoe opened her laptop. How far was Salzburg, and how hard would it be to get there?

"There are, of course, experts closer to you," Masard said.

"Yes, but I know you. I trust you, and Harrington does, too." She clicked away on the keyboard for a few seconds and studied the results. She'd learned the hard way to stick with the people she knew she could trust. Masard had proved himself to her and Jack. Normally, she favored the fastest way to accomplish something, but she wasn't about to pick speed over reliability now.

"I can be there tomorrow by noon. Could you work me into your schedule, or are you on vacation?"

Masard's laugh rolled through the phone. "On holiday? What is that? No, I am working, looking over an estate, but I would be happy to see you tomorrow evening."

"Wonderful. I also need to arrange the other tests you mentioned."

"Ah, yes. The infrared reflectography, x-rays, and such. I can give you some names."

"And costs, too," Zoe said, thinking that Poppy had okayed a trip to have Masard look at the painting. A flight to Salzburg might cost slightly more than a trip to Paris, but with Europe's low airfares it would be in the same price range, so Zoe thought Poppy would be okay on that change, but she had no idea how much the tests would cost. She wanted to be clear with Poppy about the expenses involved.

"Yes, I can give you a list of approximate costs. In fact..." he paused and murmured something in French, then said, "I must check, but it may be possible to have the tests carried out here."

"That would be perfect."

She wrapped up the call with Masard, telling him she would call him when she arrived in Salzburg tomorrow and called Poppy, who answered right away. Zoe explained that she needed to travel to Salzburg instead of Paris.

"Fine. It's funny that you're going there. The aunts went there a lot."

"The aunts?" Zoe asked, then mentally caught up with Poppy. "Oh, you mean Annabel and Agatha." The way Poppy spoke of her Victorian aunts, as if she knew them personally, had thrown Zoe for a moment.

"Yes. They had a cousin, Eleanor, who married a wealthy Austrian. They often stopped to visit her on their travels. It's all in the books I gave you." Her voice turned thoughtful. "I read those books as a little girl and wanted to visit all the places they described. I always meant to go to Salzburg, but never have. There's always something more pressing, you know? Well, anyway," she said, getting back to her former brisk tones. "How many days do you think it will take?"

"At least two or three. Possibly more. I may be able to have the tests run there in Salzburg. My contact is checking on that. If I have to go somewhere else, it may take a few more days." Laid out like that, it did sound like a lot of trouble and expense. Poppy didn't reply and the silence stretched. Zoe wondered if Poppy was about to call the whole thing off now that they were talking about actually spending money to research the painting.

But when Poppy spoke again, she sounded matter-of-fact, not outraged at the potential costs. "Sorry. I'm in traffic. Keep me updated."

Zoe's phone beeped with an incoming call. She assured Poppy she would keep her informed then switched to the other call. It was Carla on the line.

"Okay," Carla said, getting straight to business. "I have something for you."

"Wonderful." Zoe reached for the pen and notepad on the nightstand.

"Theodore Cooke wasn't part of Justine Price's life until recently. And when I say recently, I mean weeks, not months. He doesn't show up until about three weeks ago."

Zoe made a note. "I'm not going to ask how you know this."

"Mostly from poking around Justine's Facebook page, which is public, by the way, and a few other places I won't tell you about. Anyway, up until three weeks ago, no mention of Theo, then his name pops up in an exchange of comments on a photo. Justine suddenly reached out to a friend from nursing school. During their back and forth, Justine asked if the friend was still seeing Theo. She wasn't. Then Justine asked if she could get his number. She needed some repair work done."

"So Theo is a contractor?"

"I wouldn't call it that. I was able to track him down through the phone number that Justine got from the friend.

He's moved around a lot. Lived in Leeds and York as well as Dublin for a while. His current address is somewhere named Corby. He works on-and-off, it seems, installing doors and windows."

"Okay. That's all interesting..."

"But not relevant. I get that," Carla said. "Here's what you'll be interested in. It looks like he has a sideline in stealing things. He's got a few convictions and several arrests."

"Wow."

"All public records. Once I had his name, it was easy to track them down," Carla said.

"What did he steal? Artwork?"

"No. Mostly computers, it looks like."

"Hmm. That's kind of...weird."

"That he would go from laptops to fine art? Yeah, I agree. Anyway, a week ago, he dropped off the job-site in Corby. Lots of calls from his boss, which he doesn't return."

"Hmm...Does Justine have a record?" Zoe asked.

"No, nothing came up at all."

"That is interesting," Zoe said. If Justine believed Mr. Foley's ramblings about the value of the painting and decided to steal it, it appeared she'd searched through her acquaintances for a shady character. Zoe didn't know as much about the black market in fine art as Harrington did, but she did know that Justine would need a way to sell a valuable painting. If she didn't have a connection to a fence, she'd have to find someone who did— someone like Theo.

"How did you find out all this?" Zoe asked. "Not from his Facebook, surely?"

"Not entirely from Facebook, no. I have my ways."

"And I should stop asking."

"Yes," Carla said. "Theo arrived in Edinburgh and checked into a budget hotel on the outskirts of the city, then spent two days traveling back and forth between his hotel and someplace called the Royal Mile."

"It's a historic street with lots of tourist attractions. The house where the painting was stolen is located just off the Royal Mile."

"Well, there you go. But I have more," Carla said.

"You sound like one of those infomercials, 'But wait—there's more.'"

"You do realize that you are comparing my highly specialized skill set to people who sell plastic food containers that no one needs and adult-size onesies."

"Not what I meant at all," Zoe said. "You're just a bit of a showman."

"Which is also known as keeping the best for last, which I did. Shortly after Justine got his number from her friend, she called him. Their conversation lasted sixteen minutes. Three days later, Justine went to Corby. I just love cell phone records. It's like having a tracker on someone."

"Only if you have someone like you who can get to the records."

"Or the government. Don't get me started on that subject," Carla said. "Okay, back to Justine. No phone calls between them, but they were both in the area—I checked the cell phone tower data. I assume they met, because the next day is when Theo skipped out on work, left Corby, and headed for

Edinburgh. There's one text message that I found. Justine sent Theo a message earlier this week, on Sunday. It read, 'Delayed. Change our reservation to Monday.'

"So they were supposed to meet, but something happened, and she couldn't make it. I bet she'd planned to let Theo in Staircase House or give him the keys so he could get in."

Carla continued, "Justine's cell phone records show she drove to Edinburgh and arrived Monday."

Zoe pulled opened her laptop and brought up the calendar. She was in that traveler's fog that comes when you are out of your normal routine, and she wasn't even sure what day it was. She studied the calendar. "Monday? This Monday, you mean?"

"Yes, just a couple of days ago."

"Carla, you're amazing. Monday was the day Justine called Harrington, pretending to be Poppy, to ask him to find the stolen painting."

Zoe tucked the phone under her chin and jotted down the dates, her mind racing. "So Justine was delayed. Theo was already here. Carla, in all your snooping, did you run across any mention of a window repair?"

"Umm, I think so. Let me check. Yes, Justine made two calls to glass repair companies on Monday night."

Zoe stood and paced around the bed to the hotel room window. "So Theo was here on Sunday, waiting for Justine, who I'm pretty sure had the keys to get into the house, but Justine was delayed. He decided not to wait, broke in through the window, and took the painting. Justine arrived on Monday and found the broken window. The painting was gone. She had the window repaired and called in Harrington to help her find the painting. That actually makes sense. Thanks, Carla, you've been really helpful." Zoe felt as if she fitted together one tiny corner of a huge jigsaw puzzle. There was still a lot to go, but at least it seemed she'd made some progress. "Send me an invoice for your time."

"Just take me out to lunch when you're back in town. That's payment enough."

"Right. I get it. You don't want any records of this exchange."

"I never said that, but it sounds like a great plan."

Zoe hung up and went through the motions of notifying Poppy and Harrington of her plans to fly to Salzburg. Then she made flight reservations for herself and Jack because he would have arrived by then. But the whole time, her mind was occupied. Carla's info answered a few questions, but it still didn't explain why Justine wanted the painting in the first place. And why did Theo double-cross her to get the painting for himself?

---

Inspector Homes found Justine sitting up in her hospital bed, sipping a drink through a straw. He had stopped at the hospital on his way home from work last night, but Justine had been asleep, and when the nurse tried to wake her, Justine had been too groggy to talk. This morning, Justine's face was pale, almost as pale as the thick bandage that covered one ear. Wide white gauze wrapped around her head, fixing the thicker bandage in place. Monitors beeped and glowed from her bedside, and an IV line trailed from her arm over the edge of the bed to a stand with a hanging bag filled with clear liquid. Homes introduced himself, and Justine put the cup down on a rolling tray positioned by her bed. He took down her name and contact information then handed her a large paper bag. "Your purse. I brought it from the station."

Justine opened the bag and looked inside. "I don't understand...why would you have my purse?"

Homes frowned at her. "Because of the attack. We were called in to investigate it. The purse was found in your hotel room. I need to get some information from you about what happened there."

Justine put the bag on the tray then dropped her hands into her lap. "All right, but I don't remember much," she said in a soft voice as she fixed her gaze on her interlocked fingers.

Avoiding the cords and monitors, Homes drew a chair away from another bed in the room, which was empty, and sat down beside Justine. "Do you remember a knock at your door?" He pulled out a notepad and pen.

Justine shook her head quickly. The brown frizzy curls sticking out around the bandage trembled with the movement, but almost as soon as she moved, she stopped and winced. She put a hand to her forehead. "Must remember not to do that," she muttered to herself.

Homes smiled sympathetically. "What do you remember about the hotel?"

She refastened her hands together in her lap and lifted her

shoulders slightly. "Nothing, really. It's all…" she shrugged, "blank."

"All right." Homes leaned forward. "Let's start with something basic, like the name of the hotel."

"I don't know." She shot a quick glance toward his notebook, then shifted, snuggling deeper into the bed.

"Well, why are you in Edinburgh?" He glanced at his notes. "Your address is in London. Are you visiting a friend or your family, or is it business, perhaps?"

Her lower lip trembled as she sucked in a deep breath. "I don't know," she said, still looking at her hands.

"What is the last thing you *do* remember?" Homes asked.

Still addressing her hands, she said, "I remember going through some temporary job offers. I'm a nurse, you see. I do quite a bit of home care, so I go where the job is. Maybe that's why I'm here."

Homes watched her silently for a moment. She stole a look at him out of the corner of her eye then looked away. "I'm sorry. I wish I could remember, I really do."

"Does the name Theodore Cooke ring a bell?"

"No," she said and started to shake her head, but stopped herself.

"What about a painting called *A View of Edinburgh*?"

Her eyebrows crinkled together. "A painting? No," she paused as she fought off a yawn, then said, "why would you ask about a painting?" She blinked several times and seemed to have to work to keep her eyes open. "I think the meds are kicking in. I want to sleep now." She nestled back into the pillow and closed her eyes. Within moments, her breathing was steady and deep.

Homes continued to sit in the chair, watching her. She didn't move. Finally, he put his pen and notebook away and left the room. In the hallway, he caught the doctor and asked about Justine's condition.

"The blow to the head was severe, but it doesn't appear that there is any permanent damage. Within a few days, she should be back to normal."

"What about the memory loss?"

"It's called retrograde amnesia. Memory loss of the incidents prior to her fall. It's not that unusual. Most likely, that portion of her memory will return as she recovers."

"Could she be faking it?"

A nurse down the hall, who was gesturing for the doctor, had his attention, but at Homes's words, he shifted to look directly at Homes. "Why would you ask that, Inspector?"

"It's just convenient that she can't remember. Saves her having to answer a lot of bothersome questions. You'll contact me if the situation changes?"

"Of course."

---

Inside the hospital room, Justine listened for the door to close behind Inspector Homes, then waited a few seconds more for good measure, then she slitted one eyelid open. The room was indeed empty, but she could see the inspector's dark-suited back outside the small window fitted in the door. He was speaking to her doctor. She stayed in the same position, watching the men through her barely open eyes. She was glad she hadn't moved because Homes turned away from talking to the doctor then peered in through the window for one last look inside her room before he left.

Justine closed her eyes and held her position, but if he knew anything about the monitors he would be able to tell her heart rate had jumped up to a new level. After a few seconds, she peeked again. His face was gone from the window.

She forced herself to count to one hundred, then sat up experimentally. She felt a bit light-headed, but the room didn't spin. Keeping an eye on the window in the door, she swung her legs off the side of the bed and stood, keeping a firm grip on the railing that ran around the edge of the bed. She felt wobbly, but not too bad, considering how hard she'd hit the stairs after Theo shoved her in the back.

She tottered over to the cabinet near the bed and found a bag she'd hoped would be there. It contained the clothes she'd been wearing when they brought her in, which didn't look too bad, considering she'd had a head wound. Apparently, she had bled all over the stairs, but the blood had only spattered one shoulder of her sweater. Dragging the IV stand and the monitor, she moved to the tiny mirror over the sink. "Don't you look a fright," she muttered as she carefully unwound the gauze from around her head then gently probed the square bandage behind her ear before she arranged her hair so that it covered the bandage.

After a little work with the comb provided in the hospital kit and a splash of water on her face, she felt better and looked at least presentable. She was moving better and that light-headed feeling was gone. She peeled off the tape holding the tubes in place, then removed them from her body. The machines immediately registered their disapproval, but Justine had worked in health care long enough to know that even in a hospital a beeping machine wouldn't usually get an immediate response. She removed her purse from the paper bag, slipped out the door, grabbed a brown trench coat off the back of a chair at the nurses' station, then walked down the hall at a pace that wouldn't catch anyone's attention.

She stepped out the door of the hospital into the biting air and signaled for a cab. "The Royal Mile," she said then sat back against the seat, temporarily winded. This wasn't going to be easy. She felt weak and shaky, like she'd just emerged from a bout with a severe flu virus, but there was no way she was going to stay in the hospital, meekly waiting for that inspector to visit her again with more questions about Theo and the painting. Theo was wrong. No matter what he'd yelled in the heat of his anger, he was wrong. The painting wasn't worthless. There was no way an inspector would be asking questions about a painting if it wasn't worth something. No, Mr. Foley had been absolutely sure about the painting. It *was* valuable and that idiot Theo had been too hasty. Justine wasn't going to let the painting slip out of her hands again. She would go to Staircase House. She still had her key, so she could get in as long as Poppy wasn't there. Justine's hand tightened into a fist. She could not believe that Poppy had shown up early and ruined everything. Poppy had never been on time, much less early for anything in her life. She was the queen of the late entrance, so the fact that she'd arrived in Edinburgh before she was scheduled still grated on Justine's nerves.

Her heartbeat sped up again, but this time it was anger, not fear, that made her pulse pound. It had been such a shock yesterday when she saw Poppy unlocking the door to Staircase House. Justine had been walking across the close, returning to Staircase House after nipping out for a quick lunch. Her racing pulse made the wound behind her ear throb. Justine drew in a deep breath and opened her hand, spreading out her fingers and flexing them. But it was okay. Poppy hadn't seen her. And, thankfully, Justine hadn't left any of her belongings in Staircase House. She had set up in the Pinnacle Hotel nearby. Justine hadn't wanted to stay at the house for an extended time, just in case any neighbors were too curious.

She looked out the window of the taxi at the storefronts, restaurants, and pedestrians. She should have changed hotels, though, so Theo wouldn't have known where to find her. If only the ringer on her phone had been turned up, she wouldn't have missed that call from Zoe. She could have arranged to meet Zoe somewhere else, somewhere away from Staircase House to get the painting. And she would have been gone from the hotel when Theo showed up.

The cab slowed and edged to the curb. Justine would check Staircase House. She didn't even have to go inside. She could brave that rickety fire escape and get a look at the upstairs. If the painting was still gone...well, it was a good thing she'd trailed Zoe after their first meeting. She knew where to find her.

The questions about Theo, Justine, and the painting were still rolling around in Zoe's mind as she went down to the lobby where the hotel served what was billed as a continental breakfast, but was just a selection of cereals, a basket of fruit, and carafes of coffee. Zoe finished off her bowl of cereal quickly then chose a green apple and headed back to her room. She had just enough time to grab her messenger bag and coat before she left to meet Jack at the airport. His plane was supposed to arrive at nine.

Zoe sidestepped around a room service cart then slipped her keycard in the lock. She grabbed her coat and was buttoning it, when her fingers slowed and she stepped toward her laptop. Why was it open? She'd used it this morning to check email, but had closed it before she went down to breakfast. She always closed it so the battery didn't run down. The screen was dark, but when she placed a hand on the back of the computer. It was warm.

Zoe whirled around and checked the tiny bath. She'd walked right by it on her way inside the room, but hadn't glanced inside. It was empty, and the damp towels from her morning shower were still bundled on the rack. The maid hadn't been in yet. Zoe returned to the main room and scanned it. She was not an extremely neat person, so there were clothes draped over the back of the chair and shoes scattered around the floor...but hadn't she left her scarf on top of the little safe? It was in the room's closet, and she walked slowly across the room then opened the door wider.

Yes, her scarf was pushed to the side along with a top she'd worn yesterday. Zoe was pretty sure she hadn't left it like that. She punched in the code for the safe. The door popped open, revealing the brown-wrapped painting and the envelope containing the remainder of Harrington's money.

There was a tap at the door to her hotel room. She checked the peephole, expecting to see one of the hotel staff, but it was Jack, looking slightly rumpled.

She opened the door, threw her arms around him, and kissed him. His hair and the shoulders of his black waterproof jacket were splattered with raindrops. "Now that's a greeting," Jack said when she stepped back so that he could maneuver his suitcase inside the room and close the door.

"What are you doing here? I was going to meet you at the airport."

"We got in early." Jack tossed his overcoat on the bed. "Apparently there's a great tailwind from the east coast to here."

"I have a lot to tell you. I'm so glad you're here," Zoe said.

A few seconds later, she was still in the process of demonstrating exactly how happy she was to see him when there was another knock at the door.

Jack pulled his lips away from hers. "That's disappointing. Early meeting?"

"No meetings today." Zoe checked the peephole again and sighed. Inspector Homes stood on the other side of the door.

## 13

"IT'S THE POLICE," ZOE SAID resignedly and opened the door.

"Inspector, you're out and about, bright and early." The fabric of his coat had a pattern of raindrops on it.

"Yes, sorry about that." Despite his apology, he didn't look sorry at all. He stood solidly in the doorway, his bright eyes sizing up Jack, who Zoe could feel standing behind her. "May I ask you a few more questions?"

Zoe opened the door wider and motioned him to the lone chair, a delicate-looking club chair shaped like a barrel with a section cut out of it for a person's legs. "Jack, this is Inspector Homes. Inspector, this is my husband, Jack Andrews."

Jack raised an eyebrow. "Holmes?"

"*Homes*, not Holmes," he said quickly. "No *l* in my name. No, that is not a joke. Yes, it is my real name." Homes sat down, his trench coat ruffling up around his legs as he sank into narrow chair. "I did not realize you were scheduled to be here as well, Mr. Andrews."

Since there was nowhere else to sit, Zoe and Jack sat down side-by-side on the edge of the bed.

"I wasn't," Jack said.

The silence stretched out as Homes waited for Jack to add more to his explanation, but Zoe knew that when it came to giving information to the police, Jack was like a miser with his words.

"So this is a spur-of-the-minute trip?" Homes finally asked. "Yes."

Rain drummed on the window while the two men watched each other. Zoe repressed a sigh. *This could go on all day.* "I phoned him yesterday after our...chat. He was worried about me."

Homes's eyebrows lifted. "A trans-Atlantic flight from Houston to Edinburgh? You must have been very worried indeed."

So he had checked up on Jack as well, Zoe thought. She knew Jack would have picked up on that bit of info, too, but his voice was calm as he said, "I'm sure any husband would have the same reaction. Now, how can we help you?"

"Just a few more questions." Homes shifted all his attention to Zoe. "How do you know Theodore Cooke?"

"I don't." She recognized the name and felt a little flare of excitement. She and Carla had been on the right track with the information about Theo Cooke, but she didn't want Homes to know she knew about Theo. He could misinterpret something like that.

"You're sure?"

"Yes, positive." She tried to keep her expression as neutral and blank as she could. It was true—she didn't know Theo Cook. She knew *of* him, but she didn't know him.

"You've never met him?" Homes pressed. "Emailed him? Chatted online?"

"Yes, I'm sure," Zoe said. "Who is he?"

Homes fixed his dark eyes on Zoe for a few seconds, watching her thoughtfully. Zoe knew how to play the quiet game too. Finally, Homes said, "He is responsible for the attack on Justine Price."

A few hundred questions were bumping around Zoe's mind, but she forced herself not to think about them and only said, "So that means you've sorted out that I didn't do it." Zoe squeezed Jack's hand. "See, I told you it was nothing to worry about." Jack smiled back at her, his eyes flashing her a warning that she was laying it on too thick.

Jack cut in before Zoe could speak again. "You have evidence linking him to the crime?"

"Yes. And we have him in custody."

"Oh, well," Zoe said. "That's a relief. I mean, I'm sorry for poor Justine, but at least you've found the person who did it. Did he say why he attacked her?"

"No, he's not speaking to us at all. Very uncooperative, in fact."

"That is troublesome," Jack said. "But it seems to me that my wife has answered all the questions she can for you." Jack shifted his weight, preparing to stand.

Homes only tilted his head in a side-to-side motion, indicating that what Jack said might be true, but it might not. "There is still the painting."

It seemed as if the room safe where the painting rested was exerting a physical, magnetic pull on Zoe's gaze. She made herself fix her attention on Homes. She studied his thinning hair and ruddy complexion. "Yes. There is that. Poppy Foley is curious about that as well. She has hired me to find out why it was stolen."

Zoe could feel Jack's gaze on her. She glanced at him out of the corner of her eye. He wasn't happy. He was masking it pretty well, but she quickly focused on Homes. "I have a signed statement of work from her. She wants no expense spared to find out why the painting was stolen." Zoe took a deep breath and decided she might as well get it all out right now. "I'm traveling to Salzburg later today, in fact. To consult an expert."

"An expert?" Jack asked faintly.

"Masard," Zoe said to him, then turned back to Homes. "Jack just landed, so I haven't had time to bring him up-to-date on everything. The travel won't be a problem, will it? Not now that you have...this guy...Cooke. There's no reason Jack and I can't pursue our investigation."

"Investigation?" Homes asked.

"Into the painting."

"There's no need for that," Homes said, leaning forward. "We're looking into the painting as well."

"Yes, but how many resources can you dedicate to it?" Zoe asked. "Art crime gets short-shifted so often. That's why

Throckmorton Enquiries exists. You were able to get in touch with Harrington? He verified what I told you, right?"

"Yes."

"Well, good. So no issues there." Zoe stood. "I think I've told you everything that I can. I'll let you know what we find out about the painting."

Homes stared at Zoe, locking onto her gaze, and for a second she felt like she was back in elementary school having a stare-off on the playground, but then Homes looked toward a corner of the ceiling and let out a sigh. He struggled out of the chair's narrow opening. "Thank you for your help." He moved toward the door.

Zoe closed the door behind him and flicked the bolt into place. "Funny. He sounded exactly the opposite of thankful. He sounded down-right grudging."

Jack moved to check the peephole then turned back to Zoe and asked in a low voice as if he was afraid Homes was lingering in the hall, "How do you know Theo, Zoe?"

"I don't know him," Zoe said in the same quiet tone.

"Then why did you react when Homes said his name?"

"You caught that, did you? Do you think Homes picked up on it?"

"Maybe not, although he seems astute. He did press you on it, so maybe he sensed it as well."

"What did I do?"

Jack frowned at her. "I think it was because you went completely still. Not like your normal fidgety self."

"Fidgety. Hmm...I don't love that description. I'd like to argue with you and say that's not me at all, but you're right. I can't keep still." Zoe moved away from the door farther into the room.

Jack followed her. "Getting back to the main point...Theo Cooke?"

Zoe went to the door and checked the peephole. "The hallway is empty." She came back into the room, but still spoke softly. "What I told Homes is true. I don't know Theo Cooke, but I know his name. Carla found out about him. He's connected to Justine and the painting."

"Carla?"

"After my first interview with Homes, I called Carla. I asked her to work her magic and see if she could find out anything about Justine." Zoe dropped down onto the club chair and described what Carla had discovered.

Jack came over and sat on the edge of the bed near her. "So he went through all that trouble to get the painting then dumped it at an antique store a few days later for a couple hundred pounds." Jack ran his hand around his jaw, something he did when he was thinking. "He would have taken it to his contact, his fence, first."

"Who must not have wanted it—otherwise, why would Theo still have the painting days later? He'd want to get rid of it fast, right?"

"Usually, yes. I'm sure it would work that way with electronics or laptops, but with art, I'm not so sure. That might take longer to find a fence or a buyer."

Zoe leaned forward and put her hand on his leg. Their knees were pressed up against each other. "So Theo must have taken a few days and hit up his contacts, but I bet their assessments of the painting were the same as Violet's. Nice, but not worth a lot."

Jack nodded. "And since his contacts would only give him a fraction of what it was worth because art on the black market goes for less than it would through a legitimate dealer, he must have decided he'd spin a story about it being in his family and sell it to a dealer who was on the up-and-up. That way he could get as much for it as possible."

"But it wasn't anywhere near the fortune that Justine had heard Poppy's father talk about. Theo was angry and went after Justine," Zoe said quietly.

Jack placed his hand on top of hers. "So there is no need to pursue this."

"Yes, there is. I have a new job, remember?"

"Zoe, Harrington's local expert looked at the painting and said it's not valuable."

"But she wasn't looking at it the way Masard and his experts will. The value could be in what is *under* Annabel's painting, or maybe it's something to do with the frame, I don't know, but I have to pursue it. Poppy and I have an agreement."

Jack sighed. "Agreements can always be broken."

Zoe sent him a look as she pulled her hand out from under his and stood, which involved a lot of maneuvering to get around his long legs. She flicked back the lid of her suitcase. "I'm not going back on my word, Jack. I told Poppy I'd check out the painting. I'm going to do that. You can come with me, or not." Zoe picked up a pair of shoes from the floor and shoved them into the suitcase. "I'd rather you came with me," she paused for a second, then said, "but only if you're not going to drag your heels all the way. Either you're in and you support me, or you're not." She marched into the bathroom and gathered up her makeup and hairbrush. She called out, "Besides, I have a feeling about that painting. An instinct. It may not be valuable in the classic sense, but there *is* something going on with it. Too many people are interested in it. I'm going to find out what it is." She whirled around to leave the bathroom but stopped short. "Oh." Jack was leaning against the doorframe.

"So you've got a gut feeling on this one, do you?"

"Yes. So, in or out? Which is it?"

Jack sighed and shook his head, but there was a small smile on his face. "Oh, I'm in. Definitely in. Who am I to argue with your instincts?"

"Good." Zoe said in the same sharp rather militant tone she'd been using as she packed, but then her face and tone softened. "I already bought you an airline ticket."

"We can't let that go to waste." Jack drew her into his arms. "Shouldn't let anything else go to waste either...like time. I don't want to spend it arguing with you. How long until the flight?"

"It's not until one."

"Excellent. We'll just have to find a way to pass the time."

"I'm sure we can think of something. There's the castle that I told you about."

Jack leaned back so that he could see around the wall of the bathroom to the window. "Nope. Pouring rain. Got any indoor activities?"

Still holding her makeup and hairbrush, Zoe wound her

arms around his neck and pulled him back toward her. "As matter of fact, I do have something in mind."

---

Robert inserted a key into the lock on the heavy wooden door at Staircase House. "Let me do the talking."

"Don't worry. Talking to Poppy is the last thing I want to do. It never works out well."

Robert pushed open the door. "With any luck, she'll be out," he said over his shoulder as Ivan followed him inside. "Poppy? Are you here, Sis?" Robert called as he climbed the steps.

"Robbie?" A voice called sharply.

"No such luck," Ivan murmured.

Poppy met them as they entered the large living area. She wore yoga pants, a thick sweater, and held a book, her finger marking her place. "What are you doing here?"

"Bit of business brought me north." Robert caught Poppy to him in a quick hug. She managed a reciprocal pat on the back with the hand that held the book but she didn't really return the embrace. "Thought I'd stop in and say hello."

"But you never stop by. You're always too busy with your projects." Poppy nodded suddenly and stepped back a bit. "Oh, I get it. You need money. Well, you'll get none from me. And don't go to Mother, either. Hearing about your latest scam is the last thing she needs right now."

Robert had taken off his coat. He flung it down on the back

of the Chesterfield. "Investment opportunities. They're investments."

Poppy crossed her arms, tucking the book under her elbow. "Really? I thought the definition of an investment was that it paid some sort of return."

"Children, children," Ivan said, stepping out of the dimness of the landing and entering the room. "Let's not fight."

Poppy's lips compressed. "And you brought Ivan, too. The evening just gets better and better."

"Always delightful to see you, too, Poppy." Ivan made a move to step forward, intending to lean in and brush Poppy's cheek with a kiss, but the expression on her face, which was definitely not welcoming, made him think better of it. He settled for a nod instead.

"Since I'm in town, I rang Ivan," Robert said. "We're on our way to dinner. Would you care to join us?" As he spoke, Robert strolled farther into the room, his gaze roving around the walls.

"No. I've already eaten."

"Working hard to get this place ready to go on the market, I see," Robert said, his glance settling on a stack of new, flat-tened cardboard boxes that were propped against the wall by the fireplace.

Poppy picked up a bookmark from the sofa, marked her place, and then put her book down reluctantly. "The estate agent came by today. He said the listing would create quite a stir. Now, if I can just get the legal issues worked out."

"Legal issues?" Robert asked.

Poppy waved her hand. "Something to do with the trust that holds the property. I'm sure we can work out something with the trustees."

"You're selling the old place?" Ivan asked. "That's a shame. It's a great old house."

"Mother wants to sell." Poppy turned to him. "Are you in the market?"

"On my salary? Not by a long shot." Ivan noticed that while Poppy's attention was on him, Robert used the opportunity to head up the stairs that came out at the minstrel's gallery.

"But don't I remember hearing about a promotion?" Poppy asked. "You're head of some department at the university, aren't you?"

"Special collections. But we're talking academia, remember? No money there."

Robert's voice floated down from the gallery. "Been ages since I've been up here."

Poppy tilted her head back. "Robert, really. Why are you wandering about? I thought you and Ivan were on your way to dinner."

"Just wanted to have a peek. I may not see the place again, you know." He came into sight then crossed his arms and leaned on the bannister. He looked toward Ivan. "We had some fun up here, didn't we?"

Ivan laughed quietly. "Yes, that was a prime spot for so many things."

Poppy's eyes narrowed. "Like spying on me. And shooting at me with water guns."

"Oh, that was a bad day, Sis. After Mother found out..." Robert pushed off the railing. "Let's not go there."

"I'm sure it was no more than you deserved," Poppy said. "Half the things you did, you were never caught. And the other half, I got blamed for."

Robert disappeared out of sight, but his voice floated down. "Been doing a bit of redecorating? Or packing? There's a blank spot on the wall."

"I knew it." Poppy marched across the room and up the stairs. "You're not in town on business. This is about the painting."

"What painting?"

"The one you asked about when you called. *The View of Edinburgh*."

Ivan drifted toward the Chesterfield. Poppy's mobile phone was on one of the cushions. He picked it up and swished through the screens quickly.

"Is that the one that's gone?" Robert asked.

"Yes. I'm having it cleaned. It's one of Mother's favorites. I'm taking it back to her when it's finished."

"I see. You used Blakeson's, I suppose?" Ivan shook his head at Robert's tone. He was trying to sound casual, but he couldn't disguise his eagerness.

"Of course."

Ivan put the phone back exactly where it had been. "Robert, we'll lose our reservation if we don't leave soon."

"Right." He trotted down the stairs.

"So how long are you in town?" Poppy asked, following him more slowly.

"Ah—only a few days."

Poppy crossed her arms. "Sure. I get it. You don't know because you wanted to look at that painting and since it's not here…"

"I have no idea what you're talking about." Robert shrugged into his coat.

"You're not a good liar, Robbie. That's why your scams never work out." Robert sputtered, but Poppy cut him off, turning instead to Ivan. "Try to keep him out of trouble."

"Sure," Ivan said. "Good to see you, Poppy." And this time he did give her a quick kiss on the cheek before he followed a fuming Robert down the stairs.

Once they were outside and striding across the close, Robert said, "Why did you do that? No need to be so…so courtly with her. It's just Poppy."

"The kiss? It seemed to be the thing that would annoy her the most. And it worked. It surprised her enough that we got out of there without any more questions."

"But we didn't get to see the painting. We'll have to go to Blackson's tomorrow and convince them we need to see it."

"It's not at Blackson's."

"What?"

"I was able to look at Poppy's phone. She didn't send the painting out to be cleaned. It's in Salzburg."

## 14

Z OE CONSULTED THE MAP SHE'D picked up at the Salzburg airport. "Let's cut through this park at the next block. We should be able to get to the river." Zoe and Jack had left the rain behind in Scotland. With their connection in Frankfurt, it had taken all afternoon to get to Salzburg, and after a quick stop at another modern hotel located near the train station to drop their luggage, it was already fully dark as they made their way to Salzburg's old town to meet Masard. Zoe tucked the map into her messenger bag next to the painting.

"Here it is," Jack said as they came to a large paved court-yard area with benches under massive trees. "What is it?" Jack asked, looking back toward Zoe, who was trailing behind him.

"I don't know." She gazed around the street, her forehead wrinkled into a frown. "I've got that weird feeling, like someone is watching us."

Jack slowed his pace and scanned the street in front and behind them. "I don't see anyone particularly interested in us."

"I know. Hold on. Is that—" Zoe moved to the left a little to get a better look at a woman on the other side of the street. But she turned away, disappearing behind a tour bus that labored to the curb. In a few seconds, the sidewalk was filled with a throng of people. "For a second there, I thought I saw Poppy Foley, but it couldn't have been her. She's in Edinburgh. I guess I'm imagining things. First, in the hotel room and now here."

"In the hotel room?"

"Yeah. It was weird. I forgot to tell you about that. I thought someone had been in my room." She told him about her computer and clothes, then said, "But then you arrived unexpectedly, and then Homes came. I completely forgot about it until now."

Jack didn't say anything else, but Zoe noticed that as they paced on, he used the glass walls of a large building to check behind them.

They crossed the courtyard and took one of the paths that cut diagonally through a green lawn dotted with trees and hedges, passing a series of shallow steps to a raised flowerbed, then stopped because a closed wrought iron gate blocked their path. "It probably closes at dusk," Jack said, studying the gates that enclosed a spacious stretch of gardens. "No shortcut for us tonight." The air was crisp and cold, and they'd planned to use the gardens to cut a little time off their walk. He turned toward the main street.

"Wait, Jack." Zoe stepped closer to the iron gates. A pair of unicorn statues flanked another series of steps that dropped down into gardens laid out with strict geometric precision. Curving lines of blooms swooped and looped across the rectangles of green around a central fountain. In the distance, Zoe could make out baroque cathedral domes and the more sedate white walls of Salzburg's castle, the Hohensalzburg Fortress. "This looks familiar...somehow." Zoe was puzzled. Jack took another look at the garden through the iron bars then a smile spread slowly across his face. "You don't recognize the Pegasus statue?"

Zoe shook her head. "Maybe it was in the one of the guide-books I edited? It has to be something like that. I've never been to Salzburg."

"What if you added a bunch of kids dancing and singing around it?"

It took her a second, then she had it. "Of course. *The Sound of Music.* This is where they sang the *Do-Re-Mi* song. I can't believe I haven't even thought about that movie once."

"You've had other things occupying your mind."

They looked through the bars for a moment longer. "I wish it was open," Zoe said as they returned to the busy street that they had been walking along before their detour. "It's gorgeous. It's coming back to me, the guidebook tidbits. This was once a royal garden. Mirabell Gardens, I think it's called. How did you recognize it?"

"You sound surprised that I recognized it. I have a memory like a steel trap, you know."

"Oh, I know you have a great memory. It's the fact that you even knew about *The Sound of Music* in the first place that surprises me."

"Maybe I have a secret passion for musicals."

Zoe snorted. "Right. You're not exactly a show tunes kind of guy. In fact, I don't think I've ever heard you even mention a song title from a musical, much less sing one."

"I sing."

"Yes, but not show tunes. So come on, tell me. How is it that a serious guy like you recognized the Mirabell Gardens?"

"Because of my mom," Jack said simply. "She loved musicals. She knew the words to every song from every musical ever made, I think. Every year at Christmas, we watched *The Sound of Music*. It was a family tradition."

"That's sweet," Zoe said. Both of Jack's parents had passed away before Zoe met him. He rarely talked about them. "Thanks for telling me." They had reached the end of the street and rounded the corner, skirting around an ornate building, a theater. After a few seconds Zoe asked. "Does it make you sad to talk about them?"

It took Jack a moment to answer. "Sometimes, but not when I think of Mom and her musicals. Those are good memories."

They'd reached the pedestrian bridge over the Salzach River, the boundary that separated Salzburg's Old Town from the "newer" area across the river, which to Zoe, seemed a rather funny designation since the Mirabell Gardens and nearby Palace were located in the New Town area, but were built sometime in the Renaissance, if she remembered her dates correctly.

"What's up with the locks?" Jack asked as they crossed the bridge. The chain-link lining under the handrails on each side of the bridge were covered with thousands of padlocks.

"I can't remember the name of the bridge," Zoe said, "but I do remember the part about the locks. The locks are symbols of love."

Jack eyed a few of the locks. Some of them had names printed on them. "Let me guess. The lock symbolizes the love between the couple. They hook it here and throw the key in the water."

"Symbolizing their eternal love," Zoe said.

"What do you think?" She was curious to hear Jack's opinion. Romantic gestures and symbols of love weren't his thing, which had bothered her a bit in the beginning of their relationship. It had taken her a couple of years to figure it out, but she now knew that Jack loved her deeply, even if he didn't always express it with flowery words or grand gestures. A few years ago she would have longed for a guy who would be into the symbolism of the padlock on the bridge. Now, she'd rather have Jack's steady, unchanging love. Reality over the dream.

Jack shook his head. "If only I'd known."

"What?"

"Do you know how much I spent on flowers and chocolate when I was dating? If only I'd known about this padlock thing. I could have saved so much money. This is great, though. I never know what to get you for Valentine's Day. Now I know— a good, solid padlock."

"Sounds great," Zoe said with a laugh. "But we have to come back here to attach it. Or Paris. I think there is a bridge in Paris like this."

"Either place sounds good to me." They'd reached the end of the bridge and crossed into the narrow streets lined with tall buildings. "Oh, here we are, the Getreidegasse," Zoe said, taking a stab at the pronunciation of the word. "I'm probably saying it wrong, but I do remember that this street has been around since Roman times and it was the medieval Rodeo Drive."

Five- and six-story buildings packed side by side lined the narrow street, which curved gently so that you couldn't see all the way from one end of it to the other. Wrought iron signs filled the air above the strolling pedestrians. Each sign had its own unique design. Some signs were traditional. Zoe spotted an eagle head, a star, and a horn, but she recognized many designer brand shops, each with its logo fashioned into a medieval-style hanging sign. "Look, there's a sign for sushi," Zoe said. "And, I think...yes, those are the golden arches," Zoe said. "Fast food is everywhere."

"So is Starbucks," Jack said with a nod of his head at the famous sign, which was located off the main drag in a little courtyard. "But I'm sure Masard isn't waiting in any of those places."

"No, not his style at all." Zoe checked her phone for the directions. "We're to pass Mozart's birthplace." Zoe paused and scanned the street as they walked.

"That must be it," Jack said, eyeing a narrow building painted a bright gold. A banner with two red stripes on either side of a single white stripe flowed down the length of the building from the wide windows above street level to the top floor. The windows became progressively smaller the higher the floor. The words *Mozart Geburtshaus* were centered up on the building and a thick line of people waited, spilling out the door and edging the street.

"We're to pass a couple more buildings, then look for the sign with a wheel—ah, here it is." With Jack following her, Zoe turned and went up a staircase so narrow that no one else could have passed her. They emerged onto a small landing with an open door. The sounds of silverware clattering against plates and the low murmur of conversation came from the doorway along with delicious aromas. Jack mentioned Masard's name, and they were whisked through a dining room paneled in wood and dotted with chandeliers. Masard was seated at a table situated in an alcove between two rough stone columns that showed the age of the building.

Masard was a rotund little man with black hair slicked straight back from his forehead above his round glasses. He loved his food, and they focused on the meal and bringing each other up to date until the waiter asked if they'd like dessert.

Zoe put a hand on her stomach. "Not for me. I shouldn't have eaten all of the schnitzel."

"Then only *mokka* for me," Masard told the waiter. Jack ordered the same, but Zoe passed. Jack looked like he needed the caffeine. His eyelids were droopy, and Zoe could see that the time change was catching up with him, despite his time snoozing on the flights earlier in the day. When the coffees arrived the drinks looked more espresso than mocha to Zoe, but both Masard and Jack sipped appreciatively then switched to the glasses of water that were also served with the coffees.

Masard put down his cup. "Now, about this painting. You brought it with you, no?"

"Yes." Zoe reached for her messenger bag, which was in her lap, but then looked around the restaurant. It was an odd thing to bring out in public. Most people didn't pass a painting around the table as they sipped their after dinner coffee.

"It is fine," Masard said, and Jack nodded.

They were in a relatively sheltered corner of the restaurant, hemmed in with the stone columns on each side of their table. Zoe flicked back the flap and pulled out the painting. She'd had the statement from Poppy ready when she and Jack had moved through security at the airport, but no one had even looked at it twice. Of course, they'd had a girl on their flight with a long board and a man with a huge guitar, so maybe a painting wasn't that unusual. It was certainly something that a person would want to carry on the plane instead of checking it through to Salzburg, so that didn't raise any eyebrows either.

Masard moved his coffee cup out of the way and set the painting down on the cleared white tablecloth before he peeled back the brown paper. "Ah, yes, it is beautiful," he said as he lifted it clear of the paper. "Not a stunning painting like her later work, but beautiful in its own right." He tilted it this way and that, examined the frame, then carefully turned it over to inspect the back. He lingered over the sticker with the faded writing.

"A cataloging mark, right?" Zoe asked.

"Yes. The light is not good here. It looks as if some of it has worn away." He eased the painting back into the brown paper nest. "We will be able to see it better tomorrow. Would you like me to take it now? Felix arrives tomorrow morning. If I have it, he may be able to get to it before lunch."

"So you were able to arrange for tests to be done here?" Zoe asked.

"Yes, a friend of mine, who lives in Vienna, arrives here tomorrow to look at some of the works of art I am considering purchasing. He can analyze this painting, if you wish."

"Yes, that would be wonderful. But are you sure he will have the right equipment? Does he have a portable x-ray machine?" Zoe exchanged a smile with Jack.

"As a matter of fact, he does. He works as a...ah," he paused, searching for the correct word, "...liaison for a dealer and appraiser from the States. If they get a request from someone in Europe for their services, or if one of their clients is considering purchasing a work of art in Europe, he travels to where the artwork is located and does the analysis." He shrugged. "Everything is through the Internet, no?"

"Yes, I suppose so," Zoe said, thinking of Harrington. He had told her that the number of clients who contacted him through his website grew every month.

Jack rubbed his eyes then determinedly raised his eyebrows. "Henri, this has been a great dinner, but I have to call it a night."

"He flew in this morning from the States," Zoe explained.

"Ah, you should have told me. We could have met earlier." He pulled a business card from the interior pocket of his suit jacket and wrote an address on the back. "Felix and I will be here. Come any time after noon, and Felix should be finished with your painting." Harrington slipped the wrapped painting into a large shopping bag, which was positioned beside his chair. Masard caught Zoe eyeing the bag doubtfully. "It is the safest way to transport things, you know, in a nondescript container."

Jack nodded, "He's right. Anyone who saw him would think he was carrying around a new shirt or coat, not a Victorian painting."

"I suppose so," Zoe said, but at the last minute, scribbled a handwritten receipt, noting that Masard received "one Victorian landscape in wooden frame, *A View of Edinburgh* by Annabel Foley" on a page torn from her notebook. Masard signed it with a scribble that looked more like a straight line than a signature then picked up the shopping bag by the handles and waddled off, the bag bumping against his leg as he descended the stairs.

Without the painting weighing it down, Zoe's messenger bag felt extremely light as they left the restaurant. She'd even left her laptop back at the hotel because the painting took up so much room in the bag. Zoe and Jack made their way, hands linked, along the cobblestoned street, stopping occasionally to look at shop windows. It wasn't as crowded as it had been earlier, and the shops glowed in the growing darkness.

"Zoe, what's wrong?" Jack asked.

"Hmm?" Zoe said as she dusted some lint from Jack's shoulder while she looked behind them.

"That's the third time you've looked behind us—good technique by the way. Very subtle, but what's going on?"

"I don't know. I don't see anyone following us...I just feel like someone is."

"Okay," Jack said and tucked her arm closer to his side. "Let's have some fun." They wove in and out of the shops and courtyards, meandering seemingly aimlessly, but both of them were more focused on catching glimpses of the people around them than they were on strolling. They crossed the pedestrian bridge with the locks, and Zoe stopped to lean on the railing, using the opportunity to look behind them. "Nothing. I must have imagined it. That's the second time I thought we were being followed, but we weren't."

She pushed off, and they resumed walking. Jack put his arm around her shoulders. "Maybe. Don't doubt your gut. You do have pretty good instincts." He pulled her close and whispered in her ear, "You did pick me."

She could hear the smile in his voice. "Hmm...I think I remember some distinct pursuit on your part. I think *you* picked *me*. I had to be convinced."

"Yeah. That was the fun part."

A man bumped into Jack's shoulder, sending both him and Zoe lurching to the side of the bridge. Zoe smashed into another pedestrian, then tumbled to the ground, her shoulder knocking against the chain-link of the bridge, which set the locks attached to the fence clanking against each other.

"Zoe, are you okay?" Jack was still standing and reached out both hands to help up both Zoe and the woman she had collided with. The woman waved Jack's hand away and got up on her own. She launched into a stream of what sounded like German to Zoe.

"Yes, I'm okay." Zoe gripped Jack's hand and let him pull her up.

The woman said something in a biting tone with a sharp nod of her head that included both of them then strode away, examining her camera for damage.

"And I guess she's okay, too," Zoe said as they watched the woman walk away. They resumed walking, and Zoe reached up to adjust the strap of her messenger bag, but her fingers only brushed against the fabric of her coat, not the leather strap. "What—" She patted her coat then spun around. The ground was empty. She whirled back toward Jack, who had taken a few steps before he realized Zoe wasn't beside him.

"My bag is gone."

"Do you think you left it in the restaurant..." he began, but his words trailed off as he took in her face.

"No, I had it when we left. I know I did. It felt so light without the painting in it. Someone bumped into us to distract us while they stole my bag."

"WELL, THAT WAS A WASTE of time." Zoe stripped off her coat and flopped down on the bed in their hotel room. The police had spoken wonderful English and been invariably polite, but the unspoken message was clear: *it happens all the time.* After Zoe realized her bag was gone, they had stood on the bridge for a few minutes, scanning the pedestrians for anyone carrying her bag or anyone who looked familiar, but there were too many people. The crowds shifted and moved too quickly for them to spot anyone.

After inquiring at the hotel on their best course of action, Jack and Zoe had reported the theft at the closest police station. A fresh-faced officer who looked like he might be an understudy for Rolf, the bike messenger from the *Sound of Music,* had taken down the information about Zoe's stolen bag and given her a copy of the police report, but it was all done with the sense that it was a regretful occurrence, but nothing could be done about it. He had also explained that thieves often used knives to cut purse straps or even cut open pockets to remove wallets, which explained why Zoe hadn't felt the strap of the messenger bag being lifted over her head.

"What is it about me and messenger bags?" Zoe asked. "I can't seem to hang on to them when I travel..." She was thinking of her first messenger bag that she lost in a canal in Venice. "I'm just so glad we put our passports in the hotel safe. At least, that's one less thing to worry about."

When Jack didn't answer right away, she looked at him. He was working his shoes off and unbuttoning his sleeve cuffs, all with rote motions.

"You're half-asleep, right now, aren't you?"

Jack sank down on the bed beside her. "Yes. And it is good that we didn't have our passports on us. One less call to make." His eyelids had been heavy earlier, but now they were merely slits. He rubbed his hand across his face and reached for his phone, muttering, "Your credit card—"

"I'll take care of that. You get some sleep." She gave him a shove toward the bathroom. He didn't argue and went to change while Zoe took her phone out of her jeans pocket, which was where it had been when her bag was taken. Things could have been much worse. She still had her passport and phone, and she had only brought one credit card with her in her messenger bag. She had a different card tucked away in the pages of her passport in the safe, and Jack had another card in his wallet, so they would have access to cash. If she had to be mugged, at least it was only a nearly empty bag that was taken. She was relieved that the painting hadn't been in the messenger bag. Thank goodness she'd handed it over to

Masard after dinner. Dealing with the credit card company took a while, but Zoe was so glad she wasn't explaining to Poppy that she'd lost her painting that it really didn't seem that bad.

By the time Zoe had finished with her phone call, Jack, already in bed, was breathing heavily despite the lights being on and Zoe making noise. She ended the call and decided there was no way she would be able to go to sleep. She was too wound up. She sorted through her email then put her laptop aside and picked up the stack of books Poppy had given her. They had been quite heavy, weighing down her already stuffed suitcase. She climbed into bed beside Jack and clicked on the bedside light. His eyelids didn't even flutter. He was exhausted.

Zoe settled back against the headboard and flicked through the first hardcover book titled, *A Journey Through the East* by Agatha Foley, a travelogue describing the journey of the two sisters to Egypt and the Holy Land. Zoe had thought that she would skim a bit of the text then move on to the next book, but after only a few lines, she was pulled into the story, marveling at the trip preparations as the women traveled from Edinburgh to London to purchase essentials, including tarpaulin-covered wicker trunks, a new type of traveling bag, called a Gladstone bag, and macintosh sheets. Their attitude toward travel was remarkably modern. A tour of the Holy Land was considered "quite the thing" for gentlemen. Why shouldn't they go as well?

Jack rolled over, blinked at the light, then burrowed deeper into the pillow while threading an arm around Zoe's waist.

With the pillow muffling his words, he asked, "What are you reading?"

"Fascinating stuff, about two Victorian sisters who traveled to Egypt."

Jack shifted and moved the pillow. "Fascinating how?"

"It describes the way they traveled...they had to send a portable bath and side saddles ahead to Alexandria. Can you imagine?"

Jack murmured, "Side saddles? For the camels?"

"No, for the mules. And it's written in an entertaining way. Not dry or boring at all. Listen to this. 'Just as we left behind the Empress of the North a fortnight ago, today we depart from London. Society will whirl on without us—'" Zoe broke off as a snore interrupted her.

She turned pages, following the sisters' journey across Europe via train, carriage, and boat. They were quite devout, stopping to see various religious sites as well as participating in any church service they came across. She glanced at the clock and realized it was getting late. Reluctantly, she used a page from the hotel-provided notepad to mark her place then quickly looked through the other books.

The second was another hardbound book, this one a detailed account of another of the sisters' travels, this time to South Africa and the West Indies. Zoe checked the copyright dates on the books. They traveled to South Africa five years after the trip to Egypt and the Middle East. Zoe put that book aside and picked up one of the softbound books. She tugged at the knot in the string holding the leather cover in place.

She finally loosened the knot and carefully opened the

cover. The binding had come loose from the leather, and the yellow, crinkled stack of pages listed to one side. Zoe pushed the edges back into alignment as she deciphered the first entry's curly-cue script.

"Departure Preparations, June 1868," Zoe read then picked out the familiar words "a clever basket that is covered with tarpaulin, which makes it at once light and imperious to water." A few lines later, Agatha mentioned the Gladstone bag, which held more than it would appear to and could be easily strapped on a mule. Short bursts of description filled the pages, sometimes a few sentences, sometimes only a fragment of a description of a church or piece of art, other times there was only a note with train or boat departure times.

It was Agatha's original diary, the one that she had used to keep notes for the travelogue that was published when she returned to England. Zoe couldn't believe Poppy had given her this. And, Zoe couldn't believe she'd stuffed it in her suitcase and dragged it across Europe.

Zoe smothered a yawn as she tied the string around the book and placed it on the nightstand then looked at the last book. It was another softbound book with a supple leather cover, but this one was in better shape than the diary. It didn't need a string to hold it together. Zoe opened it to the first page and found the same faded pages and elegant swirling script, but the ink was darker and the pages weren't so yellow. This book contained lists. Agatha was an organized person. Lists of purchases to be made, items to be cleaned, letters to be written. Zoe's eyes felt heavy as she glanced through the pages. Reading someone's to-do list wasn't nearly as interesting as reading about a journey to Egypt. She found the list of paintings that Poppy had mentioned, three pages of neat columns, but the columns of letters and numbers began to blur together. Another yawn overcame her, and Zoe used a second page from the hotel notepad to mark her place, turned off the light, and snuggled down next to Jack.

The next morning, Zoe and Jack had a couple of hours before they were to meet Masard to get the results of the tests on the painting, so they took the funicular that whisked them up a steep rock face to the white-walled fortress built on a rocky outcropping above the town. It was a cloudy morning, threatening rain, but even with the wisps of clouds drifting across the city below and the rolling hills beyond, it was quite a view. They looked at the sturdy cannons still poised to defend the castle, and made their way through the displays about Salzburg's military, which didn't interest Zoe as much as they did Jack, so she drifted around admiring the ornate and heavily decorated doors throughout the interior, which were beautiful and had some interesting designs on their panels. "Okay, I'm ready." Jack leaned over to look at the photos Zoe had just taken with her phone. "Pictures of the doors?"

"They're interesting, and they are about the only thing to take pictures of. Apparently Napoleon carted off most of the furniture when Salzburg surrendered."

They emerged into the fortress's rather barren, but spacious interior courtyard. Zoe scanned the hard-packed ground crisscrossed with a neat grid of rock-lined drains. A couple of trees and a small patch of grass were the only greenery in the place. "I would hate to be cooped up in here for days at a time. There are only a few trees and a tiny square of grass. Everything else is stone, rock, or dirt."

"There is a well, though. Better alive in here than dead outside the walls, at least that is probably what the people would have thought back then."

"I suppose so," Zoe said. "But seeing it first-hand makes me glad I live now, not then."

"Ready to head down, or do you want to see the marionette exhibit?"

"Let's go, if you're ready. I can't think about much else but the painting."

As they headed for the exit, Jack said, "Masard won't mind if we're early."

They rode the funicular down again and followed the departing crowd through an exhibit about the city's water-works then moved with the crowd along the cobblestoned lane to a graveyard tucked between a church and a sheer rock cliff. The multi-language chatter of the tourists died away as they entered the area, and only the hiss of whispers was audible. Each of the graves were meticulously cared for garden plots with different types of flowers growing in each one and a tall marker with a cross or candle at the head of the grave. A row of iron-gated graves ran along the base of the steep rock wall, "I think—" Zoe paused to look around then said in a quiet tone, "—yes, I think this is it. I remember reading about this place in a couple of the guidebooks I worked on for *Smart*

*Travel*. It's the cemetery that inspired the graveyard scene at the end of *The Sound of Music*."

"Good thing I liked that movie," Jack replied, matching her soft tone, "or I'd be getting pretty tired of it by now. Does everything in Salzburg have a link to the movie?"

"The fortress didn't."

"And the Salzburg tourist department is probably still kicking themselves over that."

"If I remember right, there are catacombs around here—" Zoe broke off as her phone rang, sounding extremely loud in the quiet reverence of the cemetery. Zoe answered as quickly as she could and retraced their steps to the edge of the cemetery.

"Mrs. Andrews, this is the front desk. We have received a package for you."

"A package? Who is it from?" She felt Jack move to her side, and she mouthed the news to him.

"There is no name. I am sorry."

"We'll be there to pick it up shortly." They had fallen into step together, moving toward the Kapitelplatz, an open area dominated by a modern art installation, a giant gold ball with the figure of a man perched on top. Zoe thought it was a jarring and rather odd sight, especially since it was surrounded by buildings with such classic architectural lines.

"Maybe that's the point," she had said to Jack when they'd stopped to look at the weird site on their way to the fortress, but neither of them gave it a second glance as they paced by it quickly. "Could the package be the painting?" Zoe asked, then immediately shook her head. "No, Masard wouldn't have sent it back without contacting me." She looked again at her phone, checking for missed calls, but there weren't any.

"Does he even know where we're staying?" Jack asked.

"I don't think so," Zoe said. "But maybe I mentioned it to him during dinner? Do you remember?"

"No, I was focused on staying conscious. A lot of the conversation went right by me."

They walked briskly through the old town, across the bridge, and cut through the beautiful Mirabell Gardens. They had admired them this morning on their way to the fortress, but now Zoe only gave the elegant landscaping a passing glance. At the hotel's front desk, the clerk handed Zoe a large padded envelope. Only her name was printed in exact strokes on the front. She ripped it open.

"Careful—" Jack said, then broke off as she pulled out her messenger bag.

## 16

"I T'S TOO WEIRD. EITHER THAT person was the worst thief ever or..."

"He suddenly was overcome by remorse?" Jack finished for her.

"That doesn't make sense either," Zoe said as they walked along the tree-lined street to the address where they were to meet Masard, her messenger bag gently bumping against her hip with every step. The hotel manager, after a quick call to housekeeping, had produced three sturdy safety pins, which now held the two cut edges of the strap together. The cut was clean and smooth. Someone had used a knife to slit the strap and remove the bag, which gave Zoe the creeps every time she thought about it. It was still unbelievable that someone could have been that close to her with a weapon, and she hadn't realized it or felt a thing.

"How would the mugger know which hotel we are staying at? I didn't have anything in the bag with the hotel's name or address on it. And what kind of mugger doesn't take anything from a stolen bag?" She'd been amazed when she opened the bag and found not only her wallet, but all her cash and her credit card as well. Things had shifted around a bit, but everything was definitely there.

"I don't like it either," Jack said briefly. "Here we are."

The address where Zoe and Jack were to meet Masard was an enormous pink-toned building with elaborate swirls and curves detailing the white trim around the windows and doors. Situated on a tree-lined boulevard that curved along the Salzach River, it was only a few blocks from Old Town. The day was still overcast, but the rain had held off, so they had walked. Zoe was too antsy to sit in a cab even for a few blocks. At least striding through the slightly damp air let her work off some of her nervous energy.

They moved under an arched entry to a recessed door, which was glossy dark wood and about twelve feet high. Zoe tilted her head up to study the coved ceiling. "That's imposing. I feel like we should look for a servant's entrance." Zoe didn't see a doorbell in the frantic twists of stucco that framed the door.

"It might take us a while to get around to the back of this place." Jack rapped sharply on the door, which swung open, revealing an expansive two-story entry with so much going on architecturally that Zoe couldn't take it all in: a checkerboard marble floor, gigantic paintings trimmed in ornate gold frames, curly-cue plasterwork covering the ceiling and the walls, gilded accents decorating the walls and doorways, and tall chandeliers glittering overhead even though the bulbs

were off. It was only after a few seconds of scanning the enormous room that the more ordinary things, moving boxes and
piles of quilted blankets scattered around the room, registered.

A man in dark blue overalls backed through one of the
many doorways lining the entry and maneuvered a dolly
loaded with cardboard boxes through the doorframe. Masard,
dressed in a gray suit with a pale blue tie, emerged after him.
"Ah, good afternoon. I thought I heard you. This way, please."

They left the man with the dolly and followed Masard
through a series of rooms, each with more eye-popping deco-
ration. "Wow. Just wow. I know that's totally inadequate and
sadly inarticulate, but that's all I've got right now," Zoe said.

"Summed it up pretty well, I think," Jack said in an undertone as they followed Masard through a chain of connected
rooms into a room decorated in blue.

The scale and decor of the room weren't as grand as the
areas they had just walked through, but the room was beautiful, too, with more sedate moldings and a patterned oriental-
style wallpaper of bamboo plants. A man with curly hair in a
white lab coat was seated at a table in the center of the room.
A portrait of a woman rested on the table in front of him. It
was obvious that the room's furniture with its elegant lines and
subtle blue tones had been pushed aside to make room for the
portable table, which was lined with equipment. Near the
table, one of the floor-to-ceiling glass doors was propped open
a few inches, letting in a cool breeze.

"This is Felix," Masard said as the man crossed the room
and shook their hands. As Masard performed the introductions, Felix gave them both a European bow-handshake

combination with his gaze fixed somewhere around their knees, except for a few quick darting glances at both of their faces. Zoe could barely hear Felix's voice as he replied to their hellos. He was probably in his late thirties, Zoe decided. He had a narrow face and a long thin nose. The downturned corners of his mouth gave him a despondent air and the fact that he kept his gaze on the floor added to the impression.

"Thank you for taking a look at the painting," Zoe said. "Is now a good time? Should we come back later?" They hadn't heard from Masard and had come directly from the hotel.

Felix addressed the blue bamboo-patterned carpet. "No, now is fine. I am afraid the news is not good."

"Oh?" Zoe asked, her thoughts mentally skipping to the worst possible outcome. "What is it? The painting is a fake?"

Felix raised his face and looked at her directly. "No, nothing like that. Come see." His words were accented, and Zoe thought his inflection sounded a bit Italian. The painting rested on the end of the plastic table on top of its familiar brown paper wrapping. As he approached the table, his retiring manner vanished. His posture straightened, and his gaze sharpened as he adjusted a bright light so that it illuminated the painting. "First, I examine it with a...ah..." he turned to Masard and held up a pair of square glasses attached to a circular band.

"Head loupe," Masard supplied, then added, "They magnify." He put his palms together and then drew them apart.

"I understand." Zoe turned back to see that Felix had slipped on the headgear, giving him a bug-eyed appearance.

He picked up a thin pointer and said, "I look at—"

"Excuse me."

Everyone in the room turned at the loud voice from the doorway. A dark-haired man with a strong jaw strode quickly across the room. "Won't be but a moment." He spoke with an English accent and smiled widely, deepening a dimple in his chin.

Masard stepped forward. "Are you with the Hass family?"

"No, but not to worry." He brushed by Masard then moved around Zoe and Felix. Zoe assumed he was with the movers and was going to the intricately inlaid doors that stood open, the entry to the next room along the chain of rooms, but as soon as he was around the table, he picked up *A View of Edinburgh*, brown paper and all, and darted through the open glass door. "I'll take good care of it," he called over his shoulder.

## 17

---

IT TOOK EVERYONE A SECOND to react. Jack was the first off the mark, shifting between Masard and Zoe to sprint through the open door. Zoe was right behind him, but by the time she'd cleared the door, Jack was already halfway across the narrow garden area that ran behind the house. Six-foot hedges enclosed the garden, except for two openings at either end of the long garden. She caught a glimpse of the man as he slowed his pace to fold the brown paper over the painting and tuck it securely under his arm then he disappeared through the gap in the hedges. Jack was several feet behind him, but running all-out, and he crossed the distance in seconds.

Zoe reached the gap a few seconds later and turned in the direction both men had gone. The gap opened into a narrow alleyway between the garden and the next house. About twenty feet away, cars swished along a busy street. Before Zoe got to the street, Jack jogged around the corner. "He's gone," he said shortly, his tone frustrated. "He was too far ahead of me. He got in a gray hatchback. It pulled away from the curb as I came out there." Jack tilted his head toward the street. "They were gone before I'd taken a few steps."

"They?" Zoe asked as they turned back to the gap in the hedges.

"He got in the passenger side, and the car pulled away immediately."

"So two people."

"Right. One to snatch the painting and one to drive the getaway car."

Masard met them in the garden. Jack shook his head. "Gone."

Masard said something in French then fell into step with them as they crossed back to the open door. "Felix is calling the police. He speaks a little German."

Zoe exchanged a look with Jack as they went inside. "This is awful. I can't believe it. Stolen. For the *second* time. I'll have to call Poppy." Her stomach knotted. That would not be a pleasant conversation. "And Harrington, too," Zoe muttered as she walked to the far side of the blue room and back.

Felix slipped his phone into his pocket. "They will arrive as soon as they are able."

"What is it with that painting?" Zoe asked. "What did you find?"

Felix spread his hands and shrugged. "Nothing. It is a Victorian landscape." He reached for a folder on the table. "The infrared reflectography test showed the artist only sketched a few lines, roughing in the position of several of the larger features of the landscape, like the spire of the monument." He flicked through several pages in the folder then showed Zoe and Jack a black and white photograph that looked like a simple line drawing of the painting. "The depth of the craquelure is consistent with the reported age of the painting." He turned to another section of the folder. "And the x-ray," he shrugged again, "does not suggest any other painting under the landscape." He closed the folder and handed it to Zoe. "More tests are available, but since the authenticity of the painting is not in question, only the possibility of underpainting...I limited my examination to those features. I intended to ask if you wanted more extensive testing, but now..."

Zoe looked toward Masard. "So there is no reason to steal it. It's just a painting of a landscape. There's not a Rembrandt hidden under it?"

"No, I'm afraid not," Masard said. "I looked over the results. I do not see any incentive for theft of that particular painting."

"And yet," Jack said. "Someone stole it."

Zoe lowered herself into one of the delicate chairs. "There has to be a reason."

For the second time in as many days, Zoe and Jack reported a theft to the police. This time the officer was female and spoke nearly flawless English. She talked to Zoe and Jack first, with Felix stepping in a few times to help with a couple of words she did not understand. They couldn't tell her much. The front door of the building had been open when they arrived, and they assumed it had remained that way. Anyone could have slipped inside. They had no idea who the man was. They'd never seen him before, and their description of him was terribly inadequate—medium height and weight, but a little on the thin side with dark brown hair. Zoe thought his jacket had been gray. Jack thought it was black.

"Eye color?" the officer asked.

"I wasn't close enough to see," Jack said. He looked to Zoe. "He brushed right by you. Did you notice?"

"No. I have no idea. I just noticed he was smiling. He had a strong jaw line, kind of squared off. Oh, and he had a dimple in his chin, if that helps."

The police officer hesitated for a moment then made a note as if considering whether or not dimples should be included in physical descriptions. She asked them to wait while she spoke with Masard and Felix.

"A dimple, huh?" Jack was seated on the floral couch beside Zoe. "Should I be worried?"

"What do you mean?"

"Somehow I don't think it's a good sign when your wife starts noticing dimples in other men."

Zoe elbowed him. "It was a distinctive feature. You know the only dimples I care about are yours." Zoe's phone rang, and she blew out a deep breath before answering. It was Harrington. She had called both Poppy and Harrington while waiting for the police. Neither one had answered. She'd left a message for Harrington, but decided she would simply call Poppy back. She didn't want to leave a voicemail for Poppy about the painting being stolen again.

"Zoe, my dear, are you all right?" Harrington asked after she answered.

"Yes. I'm fine, except for feeling mortified that the painting has been stolen again while I had it."

"It's not as if you left it lying about unattended on a restaurant table like so many people do now with their phones. Simply inviting theft. You couldn't have had any idea someone would make another attempt."

"But he just walked in and took it. I should have done something to prevent it."

"Um, yes, brazen. But you should not put yourself in danger. He might have had a gun or knife that he might not have hesitated to use."

Seated next to her on the couch, Jack must have been able to hear Harrington's words, because he nodded in agreement.

"Have you informed Poppy?" Harrington asked.

"No. She didn't answer. I'll try her again after this call."

"Good. Keep her informed. She will be angry, I expect, but don't try to hide or delay telling her. We always keep the client up to date, even if it isn't good news. See if she wants you to continue to look for it. I think she will."

"Really? I think she'll want to fire me."

"No, I don't think that will happen, but if it does, what do you want to do? Go home?"

"Of course not. I want to find out what is going on with that painting. Now more than ever, in fact."

Jack sighed.

"Just as I expected," Harrington said, and Zoe could hear the smile in his voice.

"Predictable, am I?"

"Only when it comes to these sorts of problems, I believe. If Poppy should not require your services, then the company will cover a few more days in Salzburg to give you time to look into this theft. What were the results of the tests, by the way?"

"The painting is exactly what it seems, a middling Victorian landscape."

"That is very interesting."

"Is it? It only makes everything more perplexing."

"I've often found in these types of cases, the more convoluted they become, the more clarity it gives you."

Zoe turned her head and looked at Jack, her brows drawn together. "I'm not sure I understand."

"Well, now you know that the painting's value isn't intrinsic. It must be something else. Let me know how it goes with Poppy," he said and ended the call.

Zoe hung up, shaking her head. "So the painting isn't valuable, but it is."

Jack shifted, running his arm along the back of the sofa behind Zoe's shoulders. "And there's another aspect to think about. How did someone know the painting was here in Salzburg in this exact mansion at this exact time?"

"No one knew that, besides you and me."

"You didn't tell Poppy or Harrington?"

"Not this address. I didn't even know where we were meeting Masard until he gave me the address last night."

Jack looked across the room. "That means..."

"That someone followed us here," Zoe said, finishing his sentence. "They had to."

"Yes, your instinct about someone following us must have been right," Jack said.

Zoe fingered the strap on her messenger bag, which she'd placed on the sofa beside her. "That could mean that the mugging last night wasn't so random after all."

"And you did think someone had been in your hotel room in Edinburgh."

She picked up her phone again. "I wonder where Theo Cooke is. I wonder if he's still in jail."

"You think he followed us here from Edinburgh?"

"Apparently someone has. Who else could it be? I'm texting Carla." She sent the text, then said, "If someone—like Theo—was able to get into my hotel room in Edinburgh, my laptop was there with the flight details. I checked-in for the flight before going down to breakfast. Theo wanted the painting before, enough that he didn't wait for Justine to arrive in Edinburgh."

"But why would he sell it to the art dealer then come after it again?" Jack asked.

"I don't know. Maybe he thought it wasn't valuable then figured out it really is."

"Inspector Homes said Theo was in custody that morning," Jack pointed out.

"I'd forgotten that," I said with a sigh.

Carla must have been online because less than a minute later, Zoe's phone buzzed and she opened the photo attached to the text. She held out the phone. "In any case, it wasn't him." The man with red-tinged hair and a bulky build was nothing like the more lithe dark-haired man who took the painting.

"Wrong build, wrong hair color," Jack agreed.

"And wrong...demeanor, I guess. This guy looks grim and determined. Wrong everything." Zoe glanced across the room to the police officer and Masard. He was at the glass door, pointing across the garden. He led the police officer outside. "Looks like we're not getting out of here anytime soon." Zoe opened the file Felix had handed her earlier. Felix had documented each of his authentication steps and included the photos along with a typed summary. Zoe flipped to the x-rays and the tests that looked through the layers of paint. Except for the sketch under the paint, it truly looked as if it was a blank canvas. Jack said, "Let me take a look at the report." Zoe handed him the written report and switched to examining the x-rays, which included the painting's frame. "Well, I'm no expert, but that looks like just a frame to me."

"Thought something might be inside the frame?"

"I was hoping for diamonds or microfiche. It's always about the microfiche in old movies."

Jack chuckled. "Do they even make microfiche anymore? No, you'd better look for a flash drive or microchip."

"Nope, nothing but wood, which according to Felix is probably poplar. Here, see if you see anything."

The rest of the photos in the file were full-color images of the painting itself. Felix had been thorough, beginning first with shots of the front and back of the painting then he'd zoomed in, photographing each area of the painting. Zoe looked at the close-ups of the brushstrokes, but felt at a loss. If Masard and his expert couldn't see anything special about the landscape, she doubted she could. She flipped to the last photos. Felix had divided the back of the canvas into four sections and recorded close-ups of each one. Three of them were blank, and Zoe only gave them a glance, but she paused to look at the cataloging mark.

Felix had used a thin pointer to roll back the edge of the curling paper. When Zoe looked at the mark earlier, she had thought it was a zero and a number seven, but with the paper flattened, she realized that there was more to see, which made it completely different. Her mind whirling, she grabbed Jack's arm. "It's not a seven. It's a one. And with an eight in front of it…"

Jack looked up from the photos he was studying. "What?"

"It's not painting number seven. It's painting number one."

"I don't follow," Jack said.

"The cataloging mark." Zoe pointed to the photo. "I saw it when I first looked at the painting in Edinburgh, and I thought the cataloging mark was all digits, a zero and a seven, but Felix flattened the paper where it had curled up and uncovered a letter, a capital letter, an 'N.' And," Zoe edged toward him in her excitement, "There were two numbers, five and eight before the capital letter."

"So the cataloging number is five-eight-N-zero-one."

"No, I saw Agatha's list of the paintings last night. It was in one of the books Poppy gave me. She didn't use letters at all, only numbers."

"Agatha?"

"The sister of the woman who painted *A View of Edinburgh*." I shifted on the couch so that I was facing Jack. "Annabel Foley painted. Agatha Foley wrote books…and, well, she was the organized one. She made the lists and ran the household. I could tell from reading the travel journal last night. Agatha was the one who handled the details. She did that, too, with Annabel's paintings, cataloging them with a basic system, simply numbering them, but she didn't use letters."

"Then maybe that mark isn't from her at all."

"No, I think it is. It looks like the handwriting in the travel journal. I bet when we get back to the hotel and check the list that *A View of Edinburgh* will be listed as the fifty-eighth painting."

Jack took the photo from her. "And the rest of it?"

"I think she abbreviated the word 'number.' Instead of writing a pound sign, she wrote a capital 'N' and a small letter 'o.' See the dot there? And I was wrong about the last number as well. I thought it was a seven, because the—what would you call it—the upstroke on the number is so long, but looking at that list of paintings last night, I noticed that Agatha wrote the number one with a long upstroke."

Jack handed the photo back. "I'm lost. You're obviously incredibly excited about this. Your face is practically glowing, but I don't see why."

"Because, if I'm right, the cataloging mark means that this is painting number fifty-eight, number one."

Jack's mouth gradually widened into a smile. "So that would mean there is probably a painting fifty-eight, number two somewhere out there."

"Yes. *A View of Edinburgh* is one of a pair."

"I knew it." Zoe tilted the journal so that Jack could see the entry above her fingertip. "Here it is on the second page of the list. She grouped them together as entry number fifty-eight. She listed it as 'Edinburgh No. 1' and 'Edinburgh No. 2.'"

They were back at the hotel. As soon as the police officer finished, they had quickly explained to Masard what they'd discovered, collected Felix's bill, and hurried back to the hotel.

Jack already had Zoe's laptop open. "I get lots of hits when I type in Annabel Foley and painting, but not much when I add the exact name of the painting."

"Try using the word landscape with her name. She didn't paint many of those."

"That's more like it. Much more manageable," Jack said.

Zoe heard him clicking away, checking the links, but she was focused on the journal, scanning for any other mention of the pair of landscapes. "Two paintings. Wouldn't it be incredible if the other painting is the one that's valuable? All this time, everyone has been chasing the wrong painting. We've got to find the other one."

Jack swiveled the laptop toward her. "Got it."

"It looks the same...no, wait." Zoe got up from the chair so she could see the screen better. The composition was the same, but it was definitely a different painting. "It's darker, gloomier." The sky was gray with thick fog wreathing the Scott Monument. The whole thing had a somber feel. The paintings were so much alike...a thought tugged at Zoe's mind. She paced to the window then suddenly turned around and opened the flap of her messenger bag. "The riddle. It makes sense now. Poppy's dad was right. The painting was the key."

Jack looked up from the screen. "What riddle?"

Zoe pulled her notebook out and flipped the pages. "Poppy told me about a supposed family treasure that some Foley ancestor had brought back from one of their grand tours. The only clue was a riddle. Her dad thought the key to the riddle was the painting. This is the riddle," Zoe read, 'The rosy-fingered vista of the empress will guide you to the sister.'" Zoe took the photos of the other painting from the folder and looked from them to the image on the laptop. "I get it. Rosy-fingered is talking about the light, about dawn. You had to read Homer in school, right?"

"Sure. I don't remember much from it."

"I don't either, but those phrases that were used over and over again stuck in my head, like 'rosy-fingered dawn' and 'wine-dark sea.' They're catchy, you know, like music lyrics. I guess that was the point of them since the poems were recited. Anyway, Poppy's dad figured out the riddle. It describes this painting." Zoe pointed to the photo of the missing painting. "See how the light angles across the city? It's hitting the monument to Sir Walter Scott exactly the way it did when I saw it in the early morning, lighting up the side that faces The Mound."

"Okay, I get the part about the dawn, but the rest of it... something about an empress? There are no people in that painting. It's a landscape."

"Which makes sense. 'Vista' is another word for view, so it's a landscape painting, but 'Empress' isn't a person. It's a place, Edinburgh, the Empress of the North. Agatha calls it that in her diary. I skipped right over it when I was reading it, but it makes sense when you put it all together." Zoe tapped the photo. "This painting, *A View of Edinburgh*, will lead you to," Zoe pointed to the image on the laptop of the city wreathed in fog, "that painting, the pair, or sister painting, of *A View of Edinburgh*. What does the link say about the foggy painting? Where is it?"

Jack scrolled down to the text below the image of the painting. "It's called *Evening Fog*." He leaned closer to read the fine print. It says it was a gift from the artist, Annabel Foley, to her cousin, Eleanor Rolf. Donated in 1909."

"Donated? Where to?"

"To the Salzburg Historic Association for the Preservation of Culture."

Zoe stared at Jack. "Here? In Salzburg? You're kidding."

"That's what it says." Jack clicked over to the main page of the website, and a welcome page for the association came up.

Zoe paced around the end of the bed and looked out the window, speaking as she walked. "Poppy did say something about a relative of the Foley sisters living in Salzburg, that they visited her during their travels. So I suppose it's not so strange that the other painting is here. Is it open, the culture association place?"

"Yes. It's in Old Town." Jack entered the address into his phone.

Zoe picked up her messenger bag. "Let's go."

The Salzburg Association for the Preservation of Culture was located in a tall pale blue building tucked up against the steep cliff that hemmed in one side of the town. It was one of a string of similar buildings, all of them connected, so that the street was a long row of buildings. They paid their entrance fee, consulted the map that came with their ticket stubs, and made their way up a wide staircase with creaky steps, passing displays about folk costumes and marionettes before reaching the third floor and the art exhibit. Victorian paintings were in a spacious room with two windows that overlooked the busy street. A couple of people were already in the room, a few tourists meandering along, stopping in front of each painting, and a man in a dark blue blazer. Since he stood in one corner of the room and kept his gaze on the people, not the paintings, Zoe figured he was a guide or docent.

"It's over in the corner by the window," Jack said and promptly turned in the opposite direction and began to study paintings.

"What are you doing?" Zoe whispered. "Let's go look at it."

Jack caught her hand and pulled her to his side. "Let's browse a bit. See if the guard moves on."

"Why? We're not planning to steal it," Zoe whispered back.

"It's never a good idea to tip your hand, to show what you're interested in."

Zoe didn't agree, but the guy in the blazer was eyeing them, so she smiled at him and turned to study a painting at least twelve feet tall of a man in a military uniform on a horse. Jack's habit of always being on his guard chaffed at her, but he was smart and his caution had paid off in the past. She realized she did have a tendency to barrel ahead without thinking things through. Jack took it slower and, as much as she didn't like it, it was sometimes the better way to go.

They were about half away around the room when Mr. Blue Blazer moved. Zoe kept her gaze focused on a still life of an arrangement of flowers. "Is he gone?"

"Nope," Jack said as they moseyed to the corner by the window. "He only moved to the other corner."

They stopped in front of the Foley painting. Zoe stepped back. "It really does look the same. She captured the change in the light and weather, but it's the same style and size. Even I can tell both paintings are by the same artist." Zoe stepped forward and peered at the signature. "Yep, It's signed A. Foley, just like the other one. I wish we could get Felix to analyze this one." Zoe tapped the museum map against her leg. "I wonder if Poppy has any pull with this place? If she could get them to let us look at it?"

"Has she called you back?" Jack asked shifting slightly so he could look over his shoulder.

"No, she hasn't." Zoe pulled out her phone and checked it, just to make sure. "No missed calls and no voicemails. I'm surprised...and a little worried." Zoe had left a message when they were on the way back to the hotel, telling Poppy that the painting had been stolen again and that the police would be contacting her along with the news that they thought they had a lead on another possibility. "I can't imagine her ignoring that message. Mr. Blue Blazer Guy still there?"

"Yep. We better move on, though, or he'll start to wonder, but first..." Jack pulled his hand out of his pocket and the ticket stubs fluttered to the floor. He reached down and scooped them up. "No pressure plates or extra security that I can see. Not even any cameras. Of course, it's a regional museum, so their budget probably doesn't run to full-blown state-of-the-art monitoring."

Zoe sent him a questioning look, but they had already paused in front of the last painting then moved through the doorway beside the guard, so Zoe didn't say anything until they were in the next room, which displayed several Impressionist paintings. Zoe loved the Impressionists, the way that the paintings, at first glance, seemed to have been painted with an almost sloppy abandon, but she didn't even glance at the paintings. "What are you talking about?"

"Well, we need a closer look at that painting, right?"

"Yes."

"How do you suggest we get it?" Jack asked.

"I thought we'd ask Poppy to contact the association."

"But she's not calling you back."

"Or I could ask Masard if he could possibly pull some strings. He might know someone..."

"All right, you pursue that. I'm going to check out something."

Zoe moved to a bench positioned in the center of the room. She called Poppy and got her voicemail again. Next, she dialed Masard, asking if he had any contacts at the Historical Association.

"I am afraid not. Is it important?"

"Yes, it is." Zoe scanned the room, spotted another person

in a blue blazer, and dropped her voice. "We have found the mate to the painting. It's here in Salzburg."

"The historical association has it," Masard said, instantly understanding.

"Yes. I'd like you and Felix to have a look at it, but I need your help to convince them to let to release it to us."

Masard was silent for a moment, then said. "Let me make a few calls."

Zoe felt a presence beside her and startled before she realized it was Jack. He asked, "Do you still have that map?"

"Yes." She put her phone away and handed him the map.

He unfolded it and bent over it. "Any luck with your calls?"

"No. Masard didn't know anyone off the top of his head, but he said he would do some checking. Poppy didn't answer, which is seriously worrying me. Do you think I should call Inspector Homes?"

"Let's wait a few minutes."

"Why?"

Jack checked his watch then folded the map. "Because we're going to have a look at that painting."

"What?" Zoe whispered.

Jack linked his hand through hers, pulling up. He moved in the direction of the Victorian paintings. "We have ten minutes," Jack said as he stepped around a red velvet rope barrier that was now across the entrance to the empty room.

## 18

"JACK, DID YOU BRIBE THAT guard?"

"Yes," Jack said simply.

"Really? How much does it cost to have a close-up look at a painting?"

"Twenty euro up front and twenty when we leave."

"Cheaper than I thought, but, Jack, I'm shocked." He wasn't someone who liked to go outside the lines. "A little impressed, too."

As they hurried across the room, Jack pulled his winter gloves from his coat pocket and slipped them on, sending her a quick smile. "You know, whatever it takes. Besides, we're only looking and then carefully returning it exactly as it is. This will at least get us a preliminary look. You can take pictures for Felix to analyze. Your phone has a pretty good camera. And then if we can't get a closer look at it through legitimate channels...well, we have Emil," he said with a tilt of his head toward the empty door.

"What do you mean?"

Jack stretched out his arms, positioning them a few inches from each side of the frame. "He's taken a bribe, not something he'd want is manager to know about. If we have to get another, better look, we can pressure him to help us."

"And to think, at one time I thought you were stodgy and dull."

"Just keeping up my cover. Okay, here we go."

Zoe shot a quick glance over her shoulder as Jack gripped the frame. The room was still empty. Jack lifted the painting off the wall, pausing for a second with it in mid-air. No alarm rang.

Zoe opened the camera on her phone. "Turn it so that the light from the window is hitting it full-on." Zoe stepped out of the path of the light and replicated Felix's technique of photographing the whole painting, then zooming in on each quadrant of it. A rush of adrenaline had her fingers trembling slightly, but she tried to hold the phone as steady as possible. "I got it all. Now tilt it so that the light rakes across the surface." Felix had photographed the other painting that way, so she wanted to do the same thing with this one. She snapped several close-ups of the painting while Jack held it at an angle. "Okay. Anything interesting about the frame?" Zoe asked.

Jack propped the frame up on the window ledge and ran his hands lightly along it. "Not that I can see or feel."

"Then let's check the back and get out of here." A movement out of the corner of her eye caught her attention. "The man in the blue blazer...Emil, you said...is removing the velvet rope, but he's making sure not to look in here."

"Then our time is almost up." Jack flipped the painting over.

"Look, there's the cataloging mark." The tiny piece of paper had fared better than the one attached to *A View of Edinburgh*. "It's just what we thought—painting number fifty-eight, number two." Zoe's heartbeat fluttered when she saw several faint lines of old-fashioned spidery writing that filled one corner on the back of the canvas. "Look, there's quite a bit of writing."

The sound of a man clearing his throat came from outside the room.

"That's the signal." Jack lifted the painting off the ledge. "We're done."

"Wait. I can't read it. Let me get a picture."

Jack paused, holding the back of the painting up, and Zoe snapped two quick pictures then Jack returned it to the wall.

They were on the other side of the room when a family with a toddler entered. "I think the painting is crooked," Zoe said.

"Emil will take care of it."

They moved toward the door, where Emil was now hovering. Jack pulled out the map of the museum. Zoe noticed that he wasn't wearing his winter gloves anymore. Jack asked a question about one of the exhibits. Emil held the edge of the map as he pointed to it. Jack passed a folded bill to him under the map then Emil said, "Very popular room today. Extremely crowded, especially in that corner."

"How so?" Zoe asked.

Emil still held a corner of the map. It quivered.

Jack looked at Zoe. "I'm tapped out."

"What? Oh." Zoe had some bills in her pocket from when they bought coffee earlier in the morning. She knew there was at least one ten euro note in it. She dug it out of her pocket and moved in closer to lean over the map while sliding the folded cash under it to Emil. He deftly removed the money then folded the map and handed it back to Jack while tucking the money into the pocket of his blazer. "Two men were interested. One tall, fair-haired, the other shorter, thinner, and dark hair."

"Did they have a look at it, too?" Jack asked.

He patted the pocket of his blazer. "It's been a very good afternoon."

---

"The man who took our painting beat us here?" Zoe asked as they paced away from the Salzburg Association for the Preservation of Culture. "You think it was him, too, right? The description sounded like him."

"It was on the general side, but the pool of people interested in Annabel Foley's paintings is probably small to begin with, so I think we're safe in assuming that there is only one man with dark hair and a light build in that group of people."

"Then how could he do that? How could he even know about the riddle and the other painting? How could he make the connection so quickly?"

"He must have some sort of prior knowledge of it."

"We only figured out the link between the paintings less than an hour ago. And, why would he take our painting, but not that one?" Zoe asked, tilting her head back toward the building where the *Evening Fog* painting hung.

"A bit harder to get *Evening Fog* out of that building with the guards."

"Jack, please. You could have put that painting under your coat—it's small enough that a bulky coat would hide it reasonably well—and strong-armed Emil."

"You think I could take him?" Jack said with a grin.

"I have no doubt. You could have been out of there in under a minute."

Jack said, "Thanks for the compliment, but I can't help but notice it sounds like you were casing the building."

Zoe sighed. "I'm not going to do anything rash. I wish I could, but the sad thing is, I don't know what I'd do. If *Evening Fog* is the valuable painting, then it does answer the question about why everyone was so interested in the other painting. They went after the wrong painting, but I'm pretty sure that's not the answer that Poppy is hoping for."

"She was secretly hoping for the painted-over Rembrandt?" Jack asked.

"Something like that." They entered a square and Zoe spotted a cafe that was doing a brisk business. "Let's stop here and look at the photos. At least I can send them to Felix and have him look at them." They snagged an outdoor table under the green- and white-striped awning. Zoe suddenly realized she was starving and ordered an apple strudel. She pulled up the photos she'd taken of *Evening Fog*. She was most interested in the handwriting on the back. She didn't have any expertise when it came to the close-ups of the paint and brushstrokes, so she sent those photos to Masard then called him to ask if he could have Felix take a look at them.

"The photos sound interesting," Masard said after Zoe explained what she'd sent him. "And I will not ask how you obtained them. I will tell you that I do not need them to tell you about *Evening Fog*."

"Why not?"

"Because I called a friend who works at the university here. They have a nice curation program, which has an agreement with the historic preservation association. Each year, the association sends several pieces of artwork to the university, which uses them in their curation and documentation courses. *Evening Fog* was sent three years ago."

Zoe had leaned over so that Jack could hear Masard's voice as well. Her gaze locked with Jack's as she asked, "You're saying they ran tests on the painting? Like the ones Felix did today?"

"Yes. My friend was kind enough to send me the report. They did even more rigorous tests than we were able to do on the other painting, pigment analysis and tests on the stretcher's wood."

"What did they find?"

Masard let out a sigh. "I can hear in your voice that you expect amazing news, but I must disappoint you. It is a painting much like *A View of Edinburgh*, a Victorian landscape. Paint and craquelure were consistent as expected for a painting of that age. No underpainting or drawing. Nor was there anything noteworthy about the frame."

Zoe leaned back in her chair. "So what would you value the painting at?"

Masard made a humming noise, but finally said, "Between three and four hundred euros."

"I am sorry," he said, "I asked Felix to take a look at the report, and he doesn't see anything that would indicate a need for further tests or retesting."

Zoe thanked him for his help then hung up and looked at Jack, her shoulders sagging. "Nothing special with the other painting either, just another run-of-the-mill Victorian landscape."

"We're getting quite good at finding those, it seems."

Zoe rubbed her head. "There's got to be a reason for all the interest. People don't steal paintings and bribe guards for no reason." Zoe went back to the photos on her phone. "It must be the handwriting on the back of the painting. There's nothing else left."

"Can you read it?" Jack asked, looking over her shoulder.

"Yes, most of it. It's similar to the writing in the journal. Not exactly the same, but I managed to decipher most of those words, and there's not a lot here." It was actually a single line of text followed by several rows of numbers.

Their food arrived and Zoe worked out the text as they ate their flaky pastries. It took her a few minutes because the writing was so cramped and the flourishes on the letters added to the confusion, but as she pushed her empty plate away, she wrote out the text on a paper napkin. "Okay, I've got it. It says, "Look to the first journey. Then it's a bunch of numbers."

Jack pulled the phone toward him. "It's a code."

Zoe stared at him. "Are you sure?"

"Pretty sure. It's a simple one." Jack took the phone from

her and pointed to the rows of numbers. "I think it's a book cipher. See the three columns? They tell you exactly where to find the message. The first column is the page, the second is the line, and the third is the letter. Elegant and simple and difficult to crack unless you know the key," Jack said, regret in his voice. "Unfortunately, you have to have the correct book, and you have to have the correct edition of the book to make it work."

"But we know which book. It tells us right here." Zoe tapped the napkin with the block printed words, *Look to the first journey*. "Agatha Foley's book about their first trip, *A Journey Through the East*."

**19**

---

ZOE IMPATIENTLY PUNCHED THE BUTTON in the hotel elevator. Agatha Foley's *A Journey Through the East* was waiting for her upstairs in their hotel room. She wanted to check out the rows of numbers and see if they were right, if it was a code with Agatha's book as the key. She had sent the photos to Jack's email address, and he'd stopped off at the hotel's business center to print the photos, saying that it would be better to have a paper copy and to have them blown up to a larger size. She'd agreed, so they'd split up. She couldn't wait around for a printer to spew out pages when the reason for *A View to Edinburgh's* sudden popularity might be only a few minutes away.

"Zoe?"

Zoe turned around and saw Poppy hovering behind her. She had on a chic long black cardigan with khaki pants and a brightly flowered scarf. Her hand rested on the handle of a small rolling suitcase.

"Oh, it is you," she said. "I wasn't sure. You came through the lobby so quickly I didn't get a good look." Poppy had been poised on one foot as if she were about to step away, but when she recognized Zoe, she shifted into a standing position. "I apologize for showing up like this. I should have called you, but it was a spur-of-the-moment kind of thing." She grimaced. "I don't usually do that kind of thing, but this time, I thought *why not?* Why shouldn't I go to Salzburg? I've always wanted to go...when I read about it in Agatha's diaries I wanted to see it, and every time I see *The Sound of Music*, I promise myself that I'm going to visit, but I never do. Well, I'm not putting things off, not anymore. Funerals have a way of making you see things more clearly, you know?"

"Um...you don't have to apologize. Spontaneous is kind of my thing, so I'm fine with it, but you must not have gotten my messages." Poppy's face looked open and relaxed.

"Messages?" She pulled her phone from her pocket and checked the display. "Sorry, no. I switched my phone to silent this morning during a meeting and forgot about it. What's happened?"

Zoe swallowed. "A lot." She spotted Jack making his way across the lobby and felt a little more shored up. If she was about to get fired, then at least they could commiserate together. "First, let me introduce you to my husband, Jack, who also works with Harrington. Jack had the opportunity to join me so he's been helping me look into the situation around the painting." Poppy's eyebrows drew together in the beginning of a frown. Zoe hurriedly added, "But at no extra charge. He's sort of a bonus."

Poppy ran her gaze over him then grinned at Zoe. "I imagine he is." She put out her hand. "Poppy Foley. Delighted to meet you."

Jack inclined his head. "The pleasure is all mine."

"Perhaps we should sit down," Zoe said, motioning to a group of chairs at one side of the lobby. "I have bad news about the painting."

Once they were seated, Poppy gave Zoe her undivided attention. "What's happened?"

"It's been stolen," Zoe said. Jack wasn't in her line of sight, but she could feel him cringe. She knew he was probably thinking that she should have broken the news to Poppy more gently, but Zoe thought sometimes being blunt was better than beating around the bush.

"So it is valuable, after all?"

"No, we don't think so." Zoe went on to explain the test results on Poppy's painting and how the riddle referred to the painting of the fog.

"But someone stole *A View of Edinburgh* anyway?" Poppy asked.

Jack said, "Yes, perhaps someone who had knowledge about the painting and about the story associated with the Foley treasure."

"I saw a picture of Theodore Cooke," Zoe said. "It wasn't him. This guy didn't have red hair. His hair was dark, and he was smaller and lighter. He had a completely different vibe than I got from the picture of Theo Cooke. Theo Cooke looked...scary. Not the sort of person you want to confront. The man who took the painting was...well, almost charming."

She decided to leave out the part about his dimple. She didn't think Poppy would appreciate that detail.

"Right up until he took the painting," Jack said.

"It was only a few seconds," Zoe admitted, "but he sailed into the room with confidence, smiling the whole time, saying something about not worrying then he scooped up the painting and called out that he'd take good care of it."

Poppy swiped at the screen on her phone. "I bet he had a cute little chin dimple, didn't he?" Poppy asked in an irritated tone.

"Yes, he did," Zoe said. "How did you know that?"

"Is this him?" Poppy passed the phone to Zoe.

She didn't have to look twice at the photo of the smiling dark-headed man with the dimple in his chin. "Yes. That's him."

"He's my brother, Robbie."

⁂

Poppy put down the phone and rotated her shoulders. "That's the second time this week that I've had to call off the police. Much more difficult to do in a foreign country, but I think they understand that they don't need to pursue it."

They were still in the hotel lobby. While Poppy was on hold, waiting to talk to the police, Zoe had explained that they'd found the matching painting and summarized the findings on the analysis of the second painting. Zoe had glossed over how they got a look at the back of the painting and, fortunately, just when Poppy was about to ask more about it, the police had come back on the line. Zoe had used the opportunity to dart upstairs and grab the books Poppy had lent her. She now had the hardbound copy of *A Journey Through the East* in front of her, her finger holding it open to one of the pages that had been listed on the back of the canvas.

"So the police are backing off?" Jack asked.

"Yes, I think I convinced them that Robbie is my brother and that everything is fine." She checked something on her phone then shook her hair off her face. "Of course, it's not fine because Robbie isn't returning my calls, but the police don't need to know that. I'll sort Robbie out."

Zoe went back to decoding the list of numbers. She wouldn't want to be there when Poppy caught up with Robert. At least, they now knew that the painting was in the possession of one of the Foley family members. It wasn't an ideal situation, but it was better than only having a description that hinged on a charming smile and a dimple.

Poppy put the phone away and shifted closer to the low round table where Zoe and Jack were bent over the large black and white images of the rows of numbers that Jack had printed earlier. As Jack read off each number, Zoe found the coordinating letter in Agatha's book and called out the letter, then Jack wrote it down. "I still can't believe that the painting was matched up with a related painting with a code on the back. It's extraordinary, like something out of *The Da Vinci Code*."

Jack and Zoe exchanged glances. "Let's hope we're not dealing with something as...charged...as that," Zoe said.

"Oh, I agree," Poppy said quickly. "I only meant the clues and codes. It's like an old-fashioned treasure hunt. And I actually wouldn't be surprised to find that this is some elaborate scheme that the aunts cooked up to entertain guests that got blown out of proportion and became a rumor. It would serve Robbie right if that's what it is." She pointed to the list of numbers. "That clue probably leads back to a box in the attic of Frampton with...I don't know...china trinkets or playing cards or some other useless things."

Jack read off the last lines of coordinates, and Zoe called out the letters. After a long pause from Jack, she asked, "What's next?"

"Nothing. That's it, and I'm stumped. See if you can make it out." He handed the paper over with a string of letters. Poppy switched to a seat beside Zoe so she could see the paper as well.

"The code doesn't have spaces, so you have to figure out where the breaks are for each word, but it doesn't form a single word, at least not that I can see."

Zoe puzzled over the line of letters, but no matter how she divided them, they didn't make a word, much less a sentence. "Maybe it's a code within a code?" she asked, looking to Jack. "I don't know anything about codes except what I've seen in movies, but this isn't making sense. There has to be more to it."

"It could require an additional step, a substitution for certain letters or possibly all of them," Jack said, "but unless we know what the substitution is..." Jack shrugged.

"Does it mean anything to you?" Zoe asked Poppy. "Anything associated with your family? Initials of a person or an address maybe?"

Poppy studied the paper for a while then handed it back.

"No. I'm as perplexed as you." She reached for the image of the writing on the back of the painting. "This was the only thing on the back?"

"Aside from the cataloging mark." Zoe handed her the rest of the photos Jack had printed. "You were right, by the way, Agatha did catalogue all of Annabel's paintings. I found the list in Agatha's journal."

Poppy raised her head and stared at Zoe. "The journal. That's where we should look."

"The journal? You mean Agatha's journal?"

Poppy scooted forward on the seat. "Yes, I gave it to you, didn't I? Aggie's *first* journal of their travels." She went back to the page with the close-up of the handwriting on the back of the canvas. "This word, it could be journal, not journey."

"Yes, it could," Zoe said. The swooping lines forming the letters were faded and written so closely that the letters at the end of the word were difficult to read. "That would mean we're supposed to use Agatha's first travel diary, her journal, to decode the message."

Fifteen minutes later, Zoe put the pen down and looked at the new line of words. Poppy carefully closed the journal and retied the strings around it. Zoe had handed it off to her to look up the individual letters as Jack called them out. It had taken them quite a while to find all the letters because the pages in the journal weren't numbered, and they had to consult over the twisty embellishments on some of the letters to decide which letter of the alphabet it represented, but they had the letters now.

Jack picked up the pen and drew a line after the first three letters. "I think we're pretty safe in assuming the first word is 'the.'"

Zoe agreed and they quickly worked out the rest of the divisions. Zoe slid the paper toward Poppy. She picked it up and read the words aloud, "The spire points the way."

She dropped her hand back into her lap. "That's it? That's barely a sentence. What can it mean?"

"Well it *is* a sentence. At least it's coherent, much better than our last attempt." Zoe settled back against the cushions of her chair. "A spire could mean a church. Is there a church on your property?"

"You mean at Frampton?" Poppy asked. "No, only the village church, and it was bombed during World War II. The whole thing was gutted and rebuilt from the ground up, so if that was it, then I'm afraid the search ends here. It wasn't a dramatic steeple, anyway. I've seen pictures," Poppy explained. "The sisters rarely spent time at Frampton, though. They much preferred Edinburgh."

"Lots of churches in Edinburgh," Jack said.

"Too many to even know where to begin," Poppy said.

"The other clues were all decipherable. This one seems too vague. We must be missing something. What else has a spire..." Zoe murmured as she stared at the ceiling. She sat up. "Doesn't the turret at Staircase House have a spire?"

Poppy said slowly, "Yes, it does." The cadence of her words quickened. "The sisters lived most of their lives there. It was where they stayed when they were home. And the trust restrictions..." her voice trailed off as she murmured to herself. "Yes, that makes sense."

"I'm sorry," Zoe said, "What makes sense?"

Poppy had been staring at the floor, lost in her thoughts, but at Zoe's question she looked up. "I recently found out from the lawyers that there are certain stipulations in the will Annabel left. We found out today that we can't sell Staircase House. I thought it was something that could be worked around, but the will stipulates that the building never be torn down, remodeled, or sold to anyone outside the Foley family."

Jack said, "So they went to extensive lengths to protect the building. Were they interested in architectural preservation?"

"Not especially, no," Poppy said. "So perhaps they wanted the building to stay unchanged to protect something inside the building," Zoe said. "Is that what you're thinking?"

"Amazingly, yes." Poppy shook her head. "I can't believe I'm saying this, but the Foley treasure might be more than a box of chipped crockery after all." Poppy handed the paper back to Zoe and gripped the handle of her suitcase. "Looks like I'll have to put off seeing Salzburg a little longer."

## 20

ZOE PULLED HER SUITCASE OUT of the overhead bin and followed Poppy out of the airplane. Once they were inside the Edinburgh terminal, she and Poppy paused to wait for Jack. Their last-minute ticket purchase had meant that the three of them had been spread out around the plane. Jack was in one of the rows at the back of the plane.

"It's too bad you didn't get to see anything in Salzburg," Zoe said. She had told Poppy that she and Jack would be happy to return to Edinburgh without her and let her tour Salzburg.

"And miss all the fun?" Poppy had said. "No, I'm seeing this through to the end...whatever that is. Then we can put this family legend behind us. It's already caused so much trouble. And then I'm going back to Salzburg. Even if it's just a weekend trip. I'm going to take the time to do it."

The people continued to flow off the plane. "One good thing did come of the trip." Poppy pulled out her phone and switched it on. "It's looking less likely that Robbie was mixed up with Theodore Cooke. The description you got from the guard of the two men who came to see the other painting... well, one of them fits Robbie's description, but the other guy's description didn't sound like Theodore Cooke, so that's a relief." Before Zoe could tell her that Inspector Homes had informed her that Theo Cooke was in police custody, Poppy's phone buzzed as it powered up. "Finally, three missed calls and a voicemail, all from Robbie."

Poppy had been calling and texting Robbie every half-hour since they'd worked out that they needed to go back to Edinburgh, but he hadn't responded. Her phone rang. "Finally." She punched the button to answer and turned slightly away from Zoe, but Zoe could still hear Poppy's side of the conversation.

"So glad you could work me into your busy schedule." She was silent a few minutes then said, "Is that right? You're in Edinburgh?"

Jack finally appeared, spotted Zoe, and came over. Zoe tilted her head toward Poppy. "Robert is on the phone."

"There's no need for me to leave the key with Mrs. Reid," Poppy said into the phone. "I'm in Edinburgh, too. I'll meet you there...it's no problem," Poppy said as she watched the people walking through the airport. Zoe noticed Poppy's eyes narrow. "In fact, I insist."

Zoe looked to see what was so interesting. She touched Jack's arm, and pointed toward a man with dark hair striding in their direction as he spoke on his phone.

"So how long have you been in Edinburgh?" Poppy said

into the phone as she grabbed her suitcase handle and hurried across the corridor toward the man. Zoe and Jack followed her but they both slowed down, giving Poppy some space as she stepped into the man's path and pulled her phone away from her ear. "Hello, Robbie."

Robert dropped the phone from his ear. "Oh. You're here. Right here, in the airport."

"Been here a few days? Odd that you're at the airport." She glanced down at the rolling bag the man was pulling. "With a suitcase."

From a distance, Zoe had thought that the man looked like the guy who grabbed the painting, but when he put his phone away and smiled then extended one arm so that he could give Poppy a sideways hug, Zoe was sure it was him. The dimple was there, and he oozed charm as he said, "Mom said you were leaving Edinburgh today. There's no need for you to stay."

Poppy stepped back from his embrace. "Oh, I think there is."

"Really, it's fine. Mum said there was some sort of snag with the solicitors. I'll get it sorted."

"Plans change."

A taller man with a heavier build and fair hair joined Robert and Poppy. He'd been texting as he walked. "Sorry. Checking in with the office—" he broke off. "Poppy."

"Ivan," Poppy's tone was laced with dislike. "I should have known you'd be in on this."

"In on what?" Robert said.

Ivan shook his head at her. "You know, if you weren't so hostile, it would make it so much easier on your friends. You might even get a guy to stick around longer than a week or two."

The knuckles on Poppy's hand that gripped her suitcase handle went white. "Well, if my *friends* had better manners it would be much easier to be nice to them."

"Cut it out, you two," Robert said. "What is it with the bickering? You two can't be together for more than a few seconds, and you're at it again."

Ivan held out a hand palm up. "Sorry. I apologize."

Poppy said, "Fine. Apology accepted." Poppy sounded as if she were gritting her teeth as she spoke. "Ivan and I can be civil, but I've had enough of this foolishness."

Robert's forehead wrinkled. "I'm not sure what you mean."

"I mean this." Poppy reached inside Robert's overcoat and pulled out the brown-wrapped painting. "You should think twice about giving people hugs when you're trying to conceal something. Even one-armed hugs."

"This is a complicated situation," he said. "Why don't we sit down, and I'll explain everything."

"You don't need to explain. You and your," Poppy waved the painting toward Ivan while searching for a word, "I was going to say stooge, but I'm being civil so I'll say accomplice, think this painting is one of the clues to the Foley treasure. You stole it in Salzburg from the person I entrusted it to." Poppy looked over her shoulder at Zoe and Jack.

Robert glanced at them and swallowed. "It's all for a good cause. You'll see. I mean, it's not like I took something that wasn't mine. That painting belongs to our family. I'm a Foley. I took the painting. No worries." His smile was back, and he was working it hard.

"You're lucky that I was able to convince the police of that in Salzburg, otherwise you would have been detained when you tried to leave today."

The easy smile slipped off Robert's face. "You were in Salzburg?"

"Yes. Cleaning up your mess. Something that I have to do too often. This absurd chase stops now."

"But Poppy, you don't understand. We're close. So close."

"We?"

"Ivan and I. We've worked out where to look. It is very clever." He tapped the frame inside the brown paper. "This painting is only the first step—"

"Yes, I know all about it. This painting is part of a set. The other half of the pair was in Salzburg. It has writing on the back, a code. Got all that."

"You've worked all that out?" Robert asked. "But you think the treasure is rubbish."

"I did. I'm sure it will turn out to be something utterly useless, but since you've dragged this up, I'm going to find out what is going on. A woman was beaten, severely beaten, when she tried to get this painting. Did you have something to do with that?"

Robert stepped back, his face hurt. "Of course not. I can't believe you'd think that."

"Well," Poppy sighed. "You've done some fairly outrageous things. I didn't think you'd actually hurt her, but you might have gotten yourself involved with someone who did. Come on, you know it's true. Your...schemes have gotten out of hand before."

Robert closed his eyes for a second then said, "Okay, I can see your point. But that's not what happened this time," he added, his voice adamant.

"Then who is in it with you? You said 'we.'"

"Ivan, of course."

Poppy dropped her head back and gazed at the ceiling. "Of course. Of course Ivan is in the thick of it. I should have worked that one out on my own." She looked toward Ivan. "Silly me, I assumed you were here to pick Robbie up."

"Oh no, I'm an integral part of this search."

Poppy raised an eyebrow as she looked at Robert.

"I had to bring him in," Robert said. "He had the resources, and he's an expert. History, antiquities, that's his area. You know, I'm all about tech, but I know nothing about those old things. He's the one who figured out the first clue about the painting."

"I get fifteen percent of the find," Ivan said. "It's all legal and everything. We signed a contract."

It took Poppy a moment to speak then she finally said, "Fifteen percent?" She shook her head in amazement. "Robert, *I'm* into our family history. Did you ever think of that? That you could have come to me, and we could have worked this out ourselves? And," she flung her hand toward Zoe and Jack, "I have experts as well, but you know what? I didn't promise them fifteen percent of the find."

"Flat fee would have been better, now that I think about it, but Ivan is a good negotiator. Besides, I didn't think you'd be interested, Sis. You always sneer at anyone who even mentions the Foley treasure."

"I'm not sneering now. Too much has happened." Poppy sighed and glanced from Robert to Ivan. "A contract, huh?"

"Yes. Air-tight, my solicitor says."

"Well, let's go find this treasure so we can give Ivan his fifteen percent of some dusty stash of cracked china."

"Ah, it's so good to be around you again, Poppy," Ivan said. "You're always such a ray of sunshine."

---

Poppy and Ivan continued to trade insults as they left the airport, only instituting a brief cease-fire when Poppy introduced Zoe and Jack. Robert had apologized for snatching the painting, and despite still being upset about that incident, Zoe had found herself smiling back at Robert as he took her hand and said, "Bad form, taking the painting. Terribly sorry for any trouble I caused you."

Zoe had been a bit surprised to hear herself say, "Everything has turned out okay. That's our main concern."

Jack had extended his hand, forcing Robert to release Zoe's hand. "Jack Andrews," he'd said. "Shouldn't we get moving." He had glanced at the windows, which were black squares. They'd caught the last flight of the day out of Salzburg, and the sun had already set by the time they'd landed in Edinburgh.

A taxi dropped Zoe and Jack off at the Royal Mile. Ahead, Poppy climbed out of the other taxi first, followed by Ivan and

Robert. Poppy's voice carried back to them. "I told you, we've already worked out the code. There's no need to check it."

"Because you're so knowledgeable about codes," Robert said.

Zoe pulled her suitcase out of the taxi then linked her free arm through Jack's. "You know, I used to want a brother or sister. Not so sure now."

"They do make it seem rather unappealing. I think we'll be out of here soon. Poppy's original assessment of the 'treasure' was probably right. More than likely it's something that's totally worthless. Best-case scenario is probably old jewelry."

"Or possibly a stash of Annabel's paintings. Have you thought of that?" Zoe asked.

"No, but that's a definite possibility." As they emerged from the tunnel into the close, Jack glanced up at the point that topped the roof of the turret on Staircase House. "We'll check out the spire, and then we can head home."

Zoe swiveled her head, peering over her shoulder at the tunnel walkway.

"Someone following us?"

"I'm not sure." Zoe said as she stopped and pretended to look in her messenger bag. Footsteps sounded on the stone pavers then a woman with glasses emerged from the tunnel. She carried a heavy shopping bag in one hand and moved quickly across the close to the opening on the other side of the square. "I guess not," Zoe said, but she glanced back a few more times as they moved toward Staircase House.

"Still nothing?" Jack asked, his attention directed toward Poppy as she unlocked the door.

"No. No one." Zoe shook her head. "Back when we got out of the cab, I thought for a second that I saw a woman I noticed in the airport."

"What did she look like?"

"She was a backpacker. Had one of those enormous bags that looked like it weighed more than a person. I couldn't see her face. She had one of the floppy stocking caps that covered most of her head. It was gray and her coat was dark, either black or gray." Zoe shook her head. "It was probably nothing."

Jack didn't reply, just swept his gaze across the close then shook his head. Poppy, Robert, and Ivan were already inside, but had left the door open for them. Jack made sure the door was locked before they followed everyone up the stairs into Staircase House. They all trouped up to the first floor where they dropped off their suitcases.

Ivan stripped off his overcoat and piled it on top of his suitcase. "Poppy, do you mind if we borrow your copy of *A Journey to the East?*" Ivan asked as he moved toward the bookshelves. "Not that I don't trust you...but I think we should double check the code."

Poppy crossed her arms. "That's why you came back from Salzburg so quickly, isn't it? It's awfully hard to find a first edition of an obscure women's travel journal, isn't it?"

"Yes, it's a shame it hasn't been digitized," Ivan said, and Zoe noticed that his voice had lost its snarky tone.

Poppy must have picked up on it, too, because she said, "You sound as if you mean that."

"Of course I mean it. It's always worthwhile to make texts

available to the widest possible audience. I'm a librarian, remember?"

"Hmm," Poppy said, "Well, you're welcome to look at it." She glanced over at Zoe, who was removing the stack of books from her suitcase. "Knock yourself out, but you'll only get gibberish."

Ivan quickly crossed the room and took the books from Zoe's outstretched hand. "What do you mean? The note above the code refers to the Foley sisters' first journey, which is what this book is about."

"Yes, but we tried that book. It doesn't work. You need Agatha's *original* journal. You can check it yourself, if you'd like, but we're pretty sure."

Robert stepped closer to her. "You've already decoded it?"

Poppy nodded. "With the help of my experts," she said, shooting a small smile toward Zoe and Jack. "So, you can check our work, but it will be a tedious job—the journal pages aren't numbered—or you can trust me."

Robert and Ivan exchanged glances then Robert said, "What did the code say?"

"'The spire points the way,'" Poppy quoted then ran through their reasoning for narrowing down the options to the turret.

"So which way to the attic?" Ivan asked.

## 21

R OBERT MOVED TO THE SET of interior stairs that ran straight up the wall to the minstrel's gallery. "Not bad, Sis. For someone who doesn't like this sort of thing. Not half bad."

Poppy fell into pace with Ivan while Zoe and Jack brought up the rear. By the time they reached the small sitting area in the loft portion of the upper floor, Robert was yanking on the handle of a door set in the paneling that she hadn't noticed before. The door was stuck and Poppy said, "Let me have a go."

Robert stepped back and waved her forward. She leaned her shoulder on the door and pressed down on the handle while turning it. "This was always tricky...there." She stepped back, and the door swung open. Robert said, "Well done. After you."

"No, you go ahead. I'll give you that honor. Find the cord for the light. It's in the middle of the room."

Robert laughed and plunged ahead. Poppy followed him with Ivan right behind her.

"It's nice that they're not yelling at each other," Zoe said quietly to Jack as she prepared to follow Ivan. With the bickering between Poppy and Robert and the tension between Poppy and Ivan, things were getting pretty intense. "Treasure hunting sounds exciting and fun, but in reality…"

"It's a high-pressure situation. Do you want to ditch this?" Jack matched her low tones as they climbed a rickety staircase that began just inside the door.

"No, I told Poppy I'd attempt to find out why everyone was so interested in that painting. I want to see it through to the end, family drama or no family drama."

"Oh, I don't think the drama is over."

"Just in a lull, you think?"

"Definitely."

Zoe and Jack stepped off the stairs into a circular room with a rough wooden floor. Zoe had expected the attic to be packed with boxes and discarded furniture, but the room was bare except for a wooden chair with a couple of broken slats. A dim bulb suspended from the apex of the roof lit the area directly under it, but the edges of the room were murky and dark.

"Can't say that the Foley's are pack-rats." Ivan had his cell phone out and was using the light to trace over the rafter beams and the angle of the ceiling overhead, which rose to a point at the middle under the spire on the exterior of the roof.

"The roof leaked a few years ago. We had to clear everything out." Poppy put her hands on her hips and turned in a circle. "Okay, now what?" She looked toward Robert.

He shrugged. "How should I know?"

"You're the treasure hunter. We're under the spire." Poppy waved her hands at the roof. "Where is it?"

"For all we know, it might have been in some water-logged box or piece of furniture that you had carted off when the roof leaked," Robert said, all traces of his easy-going manner gone.

"How was I supposed to know there might be something valuable up here? We had no idea that this is where it might be."

Zoe looked at Jack and murmured, "I think the cease-fire just ended."

Robert said, "Maybe if you'd opened your mind a little to the possibility that there might be a treasure, you wouldn't have been so quick to toss everything."

Ivan's deeper voice cut into the argument. "Poppy, didn't you say something the other day about legal complications about selling this house?"

"Yes, Annabel Foley created a trust for the maintenance of this house and stipulated that her descendants can't sell the house or even remodel it."

Ivan swooped the light from his cell phone over the rafters and exposed framing of the walls. "Sounds as if Annabel wanted to make sure nothing was changed in the house and that it didn't go outside the family."

Robert's voice quickened as he dragged the chair to the center of the space. "So why would she go to those lengths if the treasure was in something portable that could be moved?

It only makes sense if the treasure is in the house itself."
Robert hopped up on the chair, and Poppy surged to it, bracing
the back of it as it shifted under his weight. He levered himself
up onto a crossbeam, sending a shower of dust sprinkling
down on Poppy. She coughed and stepped back. "See
anything?"

Robert used his cell phone light to examine the wood. He
tapped and prodded, shifting along the beam, for several
minutes. "Nothing. No compartments, no hidden ledges. Nothing," he repeated as he dropped back to the floor. "Maybe it's
outside on the roof. There is an actual spire, a weathervane at
the peak of the roof."

Poppy shook her head. "No, I don't think it's outside.
Annabel was an older woman by the time she created that
trust. I got the dates from the solicitor the other day. She and
her sister were extremely ill at the end. I doubt she was clam-
bering around the roof in that condition."

"But she could have had someone else do it for her,"
Robert said. "I say we check the roof. We can use the fire
escape."

"Robert," Poppy said sharply. "Be serious. Not now. Not
when it's dark outside and damp, too. That's too dangerous."

"She's right," Ivan said. "It would be stupid to go out there
now. Let's wait until morning."

"Or until we have...I don't know...a crane or something,"
Poppy said. "You are infuriating, but I don't want you to hurt
yourself."

From the dim glow of the light bulb and all the ambient
light from the cell phones, Zoe could see Robert's face had a

mulish look to it, but at Poppy's last words, he rolled his eyes. "Older sisters are such a drag," he said, but Zoe saw him give Poppy a brief smile.

"Good," she said decisively. "Now, just to humor you, Robert, I say we go over every inch of this attic to make sure we didn't miss anything."

"Excellent idea," Ivan said and returned to scanning the wall and roof with his cell phone.

It didn't take long, not with five of them crowded into the small space. Within about ten minutes, Zoe was pretty sure that all they were going to find were dust and cobwebs, but they kept at it until every inch of the attic had been examined.

As they tapped and poked and prodded their way through the final sections, Jack, who was standing beside Robert, said, "So I assume it was you two," he glanced from Robert to Ivan, "who took Zoe's bag in Salzburg." He made it a statement, not a question.

Robert shrugged one shoulder. "Not my finest hour, but we knew you were taking the painting to the art dealer. We missed you at your hotel—"

"So you stole my messenger bag after dinner, thinking it had the painting in it," Zoe said.

Robert looked down at the floor. "Yes, it was wrong. I completely apologize. I hope I didn't hurt you when I bumped into you. I didn't mean to knock you to the ground, only to throw you off balance. I felt terrible, I really did."

"I bet you did, especially when you realized the painting wasn't in the bag."

Robert sighed. "Yes, that was a low point for us." He glanced at Ivan.

Ivan ran his hand over his eyes. While Robert merely looked like he was sorry that he'd gotten caught, Ivan looked truly pained. "I'm sorry," Ivan said. "We got swept up in the hunt. It was wrong. We shouldn't have done it, even though the painting belonged to Robert's family. We shouldn't have swiped it from you."

"But we had our reasons," Robert said quickly. "We didn't know you." He pointed to Jack and Zoe. "You might have received the information from your art expert person and disappeared. We couldn't take that chance. We didn't have any other choice but to watch your hotel and follow you the next day. We knew you'd have to pick up the painting from the art dealer at some point."

"But how did you even know we were in Salzburg?" Zoe asked.

Ivan looked quickly at Poppy then away. "I—ah—saw a message on Poppy's phone."

Poppy had been looking at a portion of the roof, but she turned quickly, an angry look on her face. "The night you came to ask about the painting."

Robert said quickly, "Water under the bridge. We're at this point now. We shouldn't focus on what happened days ago. We have to concentrate on moving forward."

"Yes," Ivan said. "I don't want to cause trouble, but I think we should reexamine the meaning of the word 'spire.'" He sent a worried look toward Poppy. "I think your reasoning is good, but there's nothing here." He waved the beam of light from his cell phone around. "And I think you're right about the chance of something being on the exterior of the roof—that's a long shot."

"Go on," Poppy said. "I'm all for a new theory."

Robert stopped tapping on a beam and looked toward Ivan as well. "If we're back to assuming it refers to some church spire, then it could take us years to work our way through all the churches in Edinburgh."

Zoe turned slowly away from the area she had been tapping on. "But that's so broad. If someone went to all the trouble of leaving the clues and the code, then surely they meant for them to lead to a definite conclusion."

"Unless they had a sadistic streak," Poppy said.

Ivan said, "No, she's right. We're missing something. We just have to work out what it is. The word spire has to refer to a specific spire, not just any spire in Edinburgh."

"There's the spire in the paintings," Robert said, his voice quickening. "The Scott Monument. It's prominent in both paintings."

Poppy wrinkled her forehead as she shook his head. "You think a little old lady hid something in the Scott Monument? You've seen it. There's nothing there but stone and mortar."

"But there are crevices and niches. It could be tucked away there."

Ivan shook his head. "It's a public place. Risky to leave something where anyone might discover it."

"Especially if she went to the trouble of setting up the trust for this building," Jack added.

"As far as Staircase House, there are no other spires here

except in pictures," Robert said as he headed for the stairs. "Tomorrow I'll go out on the roof."

"No spires except in the pictures," Zoe murmured to herself, her thoughts racing. She turned toward Jack, gripped his arm. "The spire is in the painting."

She turned eagerly back to the group, but Jack put a hand on her arm. "I think they've almost worked it out for themselves."

"The painting. Oh! The spire in the painting," Poppy said, "Of course, that's it. It's not a physical structure, Robbie. The spire in the painting points the way."

Robert frowned at her, then his face changed, relaxing into a smile. "How could we be so dense?"

Ivan glanced between the brother and sister. "I'm afraid you'll have to clue me in here because I'm lost."

"Of the two paintings in the set Annabel painted, only one had a visible spire, *A View of Edinburgh*," Robert said. "In the other painting, fog covers the spire of the Scott Monument."

"*A View of Edinburgh* has hung in the same place for years," Poppy said moving toward the stairs, her voice quickening with excitement. "Probably since Annabel and Agatha lived here. I've looked at some photos from Edwardian times, and all those paintings in the sitting area of the minstrel's gallery were as they are now."

"As they were until a few days ago," Robert added.

Ivan and Robert thundered down the stairs after Poppy. Jack and Zoe followed more slowly. Zoe said, "You wanted them to have the thrill of figuring it out."

Jack shrugged one shoulder. "Solving a puzzle together is a pretty good way to strengthen a relationship."

Zoe smiled back at him, thinking of the puzzles they'd untangled together. It had brought them closer—rejuvenated their nearly dead relationship, in fact.

When they emerged into the sitting area of the minstrel's gallery, Poppy, Ivan, and Robert were all gathered around the area of paneling where the landscape painting had hung.

"There's a seam here." Ivan traced his hand along a section of paneling above the empty space on the wall. "Got a knife or something thin?"

Poppy went to a small desk in the corner and opened a drawer. "Would a letter opener work?"

"Perfect." Ivan inserted the thin blade in the space between two sections of paneling and worked it back and forth.

"Careful," Poppy said. "Mum will not be happy if we destroy antique paneling."

The wood flexed then came away from the wall, revealing an alcove about four inches high and eight inches long. "Shine a light in there," Poppy said, but Robert reached in. "Oh, Robbie. No. There might be bugs or mice or—" She broke off as Robert pulled out a wooden box slightly smaller than the opening.

It must have been heavy because he used two hands to transfer it to the coffee table in the sitting area. They all moved as a group to circle the table. Zoe shot a look at Jack, widening her eyes. The atmosphere had changed, shifting away from excited anticipation. Now tension vibrated through the group.

Poppy ran her hand gently over the elaborate carving on the outside of the box. "It looks Oriental."

"Go on, open it," Robbie said. "It's not Pandora's box."

Poppy pulled her hand away. "I'm not so sure." She stepped back. "You do it. You were the one who always believed in the treasure."

"Don't worry, Sis. It's just a box, no curse." He unhooked the ornate leather latch then flipped the box open.

Zoe got a glimpse of fabric inside the box before she heard a sudden in-take of breath, and a flurry of movement near Poppy made everyone look up.

"Don't even think about moving," Justine said. She had one arm looped around Poppy and had a chef's knife pressed to Poppy's throat.

## 22

"EVERYTHING WILL BE FINE IF you all do exactly what I say." Justine's voice was smooth with an almost singsong quality to it. "I don't want to hurt anyone."

Zoe thought that was quite a statement for someone to make while holding a knife to another person's throat, but she kept silent. Poppy's frightened gaze skittered around the group, but she held the rest of her body completely still. She had her head angled back as far from the knife as she could, but the silver edge of the huge blade pressed into Poppy's throat under her jaw, leaving a long indention in her pale skin. Zoe looked around quickly to see if there was anyone else with Justine, like a large man with red hair—could he have gotten out of jail, made bail somehow—but Theo Cooke was nowhere in sight.

Zoe eyed the window with the fire escape, but it was closed. Then she shot a quick glance down over the railing into the main room below, but the doors and windows all appeared to be shut. Then she remembered her theory that Justine had a key to Staircase House. She must have unlocked the front door, just as she had the first time Zoe met her when she'd been pretending to be Poppy. She'd slipped inside while they were all in the attic. She must have grabbed the knife from the kitchen then waited until they'd pulled the box out of its hiding place before sneaking up on Poppy. They'd all been so focused on the box that they hadn't noticed Justine moving in on the group.

Robert took a step toward the women, and Justine moved back, dragging Poppy with her, pressing the knife deeper into her skin. "Stay back, Robert. I'll have no foolishness. Remember, I'm a nurse. I know exactly where to cut her."

Robert immediately held up his hands, palms out. "Fine. Right. No one is moving. See, we're all standing still. But there's no need for this." He leaned toward her and lowered his voice slightly as if he were sharing a secret with her. "Justine, isn't it?" She nodded her head sharply once, and Robert pulled back, a wide smile on his face. "I thought I recognized you. You're the one who took such good care of my father. Look, you can lose the knife. Just tell us what you want. It will all be fine."

Zoe and Jack were standing beside each other, their arms touching. She looked at him out of the corner of her eye. He gave a tiny shake of his head, and she knew he was conveying *not yet*. Their hands were each at their sides and she moved her fingers a bit so that her fingers slid into his palm. She squeezed his hand.

"You can drop the friendly act," Justine said, "And forget

flashing your charming smile. It won't work. You'll save us a lot of time, if you do as I say. I know that this is the only way to get what I want." Justine's fingers on the knife handle flexed and tightened. Poppy sucked in a breath.

"Okay. You're the boss," Robert said, his smile still firmly in place, but Zoe could see the rise and fall of his chest through his shirt. He was breathing like he'd finished a sprint.

Justine tilted her chin toward the box. "Take it out. Unwrap it." Robert leaned down and pulled the fabric away. At first Zoe thought it was another wooden box inside because whatever was in there was the same dark brown color as the wood, but then she realized it wasn't wood, but aged leather. Robert pushed the fabric farther away, revealing the uneven edges of pages.

"It's a...book?" Justine said, her tone incredulous. "I chased you all over blooming Europe for a book?"

Zoe looked at Justine and, since Zoe had shifted her attention away from the knife blade, she noticed a knitted gray stocking cap half-tucked into one of Justine's pockets. "You were the backpacker I saw in the airport. You were also in Salzburg..." Zoe paused, working it out. "And I saw you another time, too. At the Mirabell Gardens. You didn't have the hat then, but you were following us." Zoe glanced at Jack. "Remember, I thought for a second I had seen Poppy, but it was you, wasn't it?"

Justine only gave Zoe a quick glance out of the corner of her eye, and didn't respond to Zoe. Justine refocused on the book. "Go on, open it," she directed Robert.

He reached for the cover, but Ivan stretched out a hand and took a half step forward. "Careful. It will be delicate."

"Quiet," Justine said, and Zoe noticed her voice had lost its singsong quality and was edging into shrillness.

"He's a book expert. Librarian," Robert said easily as he slowly lifted the cover. "There's a piece of paper here. Looks like a letter. Old-fashioned hand."

"Forget the letter. What's inside the book?" Justine asked. "It's probably just a hiding place."

Poppy spoke for the first time. "Give her the book, Robert. Take it, Justine. Just take it, and walk away. We'll forget the whole thing."

Justine tightened her arm and pressed the knife deeper into Poppy's throat. "I don't want a book. I want the treasure."

Robert removed the letter, which was folded. He set it on the table without opening it then delicately fanned the pages of the book. "It's—ah, it looks like it is a book."

From where Zoe was standing, she could see that writing in black ink dominated the pages, but another text in a faded light-brown color was interspersed between the dark black text.

Justine cursed under her breath, and Ivan said quickly, "But it could be a very valuable book." He stared at the pages. "May I?"

Justine frowned, and Robert said, "Like I said, Ivan needs to look at it. Books are his thing. Head Librarian."

Ivan didn't look away from the book as he said, "Antiquarian books are my specialty."

"Fine," Justine said, "Hand it to him. Be quick about it. No, stay apart. Just reach out and hand it to him."

Robert extended the book, and Ivan took it. Ivan sent Poppy a quick look before focusing on the heavy volume in his hand. He fingered the texture of the pages and examined the writing on a few of them, then looked up. "I can't be sure, not without tests and extensive study, but it is extremely old. It's actually parchment—animal skin, not paper—and the writing is Greek—"

"I don't care about all that," Justine said impatiently, and Poppy sucked in an unsteady breath as the knife grooved deeper into her neck. Zoe's stomach clenched as she watched, afraid that she was about to see blood.

Justine said, "I only care about—"

"Yes, the treasure. We know, but if you'll listen a moment, I'll explain. The Greek writing is what makes it valuable," Ivan said, overriding Justine. "The book is a palimpsest." He tilted it so that Justine could see the pages. "See these faded letters?" He pointed to the dim outline of light brown letters that covered the page under the thick strokes of the dark ink. "It's called an undertext, also in what I believe is Greek. Books were rare and hard to come by in the ancient world, even in the first century. Often, the original text of a book was scraped off and the book was reused with new writing on top. That's what has happened here."

"And that makes it worth money?" Justine said slowly, her tone suspicious.

"Yes," Ivan said, his gaze going to Poppy. Zoe noticed that

Ivan was quite pale and that his hand shook as he repositioned the heavy book in his palm.

"How much?"

"Well...a library recently raised a million pounds to keep a book like this, a codex, in its collection."

Justine licked her lips.

He closed the book and held it out. "Here. Take it." He extended his other arm to Poppy. "Just let Poppy go. You can walk out of here, just as she said. We won't stop you." Ivan flexed his fingers as if he could draw Poppy to him.

"No," Justine said sharply, and Zoe tensed. She felt Jack shift his feet slightly, and Zoe knew he was poised to move. It gave her a sick feeling in the pit of her stomach, the thought of him charging Justine with her long knife.

"Here's what you're going to do," Justine said. "You put that book down there on the fabric on the table and back up. All of you, back up." Ivan moved slowly and put the book down as Justine had instructed. "You back away, too, Robert. No, another step. Good. Now," Justine looked toward Zoe, "You. When I tell you, wrap the fabric around the book and hand it to me."

Jack gave her hand two quick squeezes, and Zoe's insides surged. It was a signal. Jack was going to do something. Zoe stepped to the table and wrapped the book in the fabric.

"I want you to hand it to me, slow and easy," Justine said. "Then Poppy and I will go down the stairs together." She tilted her head, indicating the set of stairs against the wall that opened into the main floor below. "If you're all good little boys and girls and stay here, when I get to the bottom of the steps,

I'll let Poppy go, alive. I get to disappear, and she gets to live. Everyone understand?"

The tense group nodded.

Justine motioned her chin at Zoe. "Go on."

Zoe inched forward and wrapped the fabric, some sort of shawl, she realized as she handled it, tightly around the book.

Justine said, "Not like that. Looser, so that I have something to hold onto. Yes, better. Now, slowly hand it over."

Zoe gathered the corners of the fabric together and lifted it from the table, holding it like those old illustrations of a stork delivering a baby in a swath of fabric held in its beak. Zoe extended the bundle toward Justine. At the edge of her vision, she could see Robert tense as Justine reached out her free hand. A second before Justine's fingers closed around the fabric, Zoe let it slip through her fingers. The book tumbled out, and the three men converged on Justine.

It was over in seconds. Almost before Zoe blinked, Jack had twisted Justine's arm away and forced her to drop the knife. It clattered to the floor, narrowly missing the book. Robert tackled Justine, knocking her away from Poppy and out of reach of the knife. Ivan pulled Poppy away from Justine and into his arms.

It took considerably longer for the police to arrive, and longer still for Inspector Homes to arrive, but once he was in Staircase House and heard the full story of what had happened, he bagged the knife, which Jack had prevented anyone from touching, and had Justine escorted away to await charges. "Since you were feeling well enough to leave the hospital," he said to her before an officer escorted her out, "I'm sure you'll finally be able to finish our little chat."

Once Justine had left the premises, Zoe relaxed and everyone else appeared to breathe easier, too.

"So, this is all about a book?" Homes asked, looking toward the coffee table where Ivan had placed the book, which was now nestled in the scarf. Ivan described what he had told Justine about the book.

"Sergeant Malone will enjoy this one," Homes murmured in an undertone, a slight smile on his face. Jack looked at Zoe questioningly. She shrugged and mouthed, "No idea."

An officer entered the main room below and called up to Homes, saying he was needed. Homes said he'd be with him in a moment then turned back to them. "I will need statements from all of you, but I think that can wait until tomorrow. You can rest easy. Justine will not be able to leave our custody, and the other man who caused so much trouble, Cooke, is still detained."

As Homes trotted down the staircase to the main room, Robert slapped Ivan on the back. "Good show, mate, coming up with the story about the book. Ancient Greek, indeed."

"I never said it was ancient Greek. In all likelihood it is written in Koine Greek, but you'll need to consult a linguistics expert."

Robert's always-ready smile faded. "You mean you were serious? The book is a...what did you call it?"

"A palimpsest. Yes, I was completely serious. It could be extremely valuable."

Robert plopped into a chair.

While Poppy had moved out of Ivan's arms once the police arrived, Zoe noticed that Poppy had remained close to him. She dropped down to her knees by the coffee table and ran her finger along the edge of the book, then lifted the cover an inch to look at the inside. "You were going to hand this over to Justine...for me?" Poppy looked up at Ivan.

He smiled down at her. "Of course."

"Are you crazy? What were you thinking?"" Robert asked then noticed the lingering gaze that Poppy and Ivan were exchanging. "Oh—it's like that, is it? I thought she drove you crazy."

Ivan smiled. "She does."

A blush filled Poppy's cheeks.

Zoe whispered to Jack, "Well, that's a turn I didn't expect."

Jack shrugged a shoulder and said quietly, "I guess it's true, that saying about the opposite of love. It isn't hate, but indifference."

Zoe tilted her head back and forth, thinking over their own relationship. "I'd have to agree that I never felt indifferent toward you. You did drive me crazy. Still do in fact. Speaking of driving me crazy, I can't believe you rushed Justine. We need to have a chat about reasonable actions. You're supposed to be the measured, thoughtful one in this relationship."

"Oh, come on. You'd no more standby and let her get hurt than I would. You did your part creating the distraction quite nicely."

"Just don't do anything like that again, okay? We're going back to Dallas, and you're going to consult with clients about their security systems, a nice safe job."

Jack looked up at the ceiling. "Fine. And in a few weeks you'll be bored out of your mind, longing for another assignment from Harrington."

Zoe had to laugh. "You're probably right."

"And you," Robert finally found his voice as he looked to Poppy. "You hate him. Always have. Ever since I brought him home that summer."

"Yes, I suppose it started then."

Robert rolled his eyes and reached for the book. "I hope I never fall in love. Turns people into blithering idiots. As in this case, here we have a book possibly worth a million pounds, and you two can't stop gazing at each other to look at it or at this letter." Robert plucked the delicate paper from the table where it had fallen. "I don't know a thing about old books, but I know this isn't ancient Greek. I still can't read it, though."

"Koine," Ivan corrected.

Zoe peered over his shoulder. "That looks similar to the handwriting in the journal."

"Here let me see." Poppy dragged her gaze away from Ivan and perched on the arm of Robert's chair. "No, I don't think this is Agatha's handwriting. It has more loops and embellishments. Perhaps it is Annabell's handwriting." Poppy looked at the date at the top. "Yes, it was written...um...I'd have to check the dates, but I think it was right before she died." She flipped it over to the back.

"That does look like the signature on Annabel's paintings," Zoe said.

"It does, doesn't it?" Poppy turned back to the beginning of the letter. "Let me see if I can make it out. It is addressed to 'Whomever shall find this precious book.'"

"Go on," Robert said. "What's this word here? I can't make it out."

Poppy batted his hand away and focused on the letter. She read, "'My sister, Agatha, and I brought this book back from one of our travels. We have an interest in all things devout and Holy and, being assured it was a copy of one of the gospels, we —of course—bought it. We purchased it from a little stall in Cairo along with a few other sacred items. We both felt that it was our duty to look after these precious things lest they be lost to someone who would not care for them or respect them. However, upon our return from our travels, we had difficulty convincing anyone of repute to examine it, for we are only women and what can women know of important relics? Years passed, and I am rather ashamed to say that this book lost its place in our thoughts. We grew quite busy with our own inter-ests. Unencumbered by spouse or children—which we longed for, but because we were not so blessed—we pursued our interests. Travel, which we jointly delighted in as well as Agatha in her writing and books, and me in my paintings.

"'Of course, we treated the book carefully, always keeping it dry and secure in the box we had made for it in Egypt, but it was only when we made the acquaintance of a certain doctor of Oriental studies from Cambridge within the last fortnight that it again became the focus of our attention. As we believed, it was indeed something of great importance. Unfortunately, our so-called friend proved to be exceedingly greedy. I will not list his name here for "vengeance is mine, saith the Lord." It is not our place to judge him. His perfidy was his undoing. His actions, while disloyal, did reveal to us the incredible worth of this book. I am glad that Agatha knew the real value of it. It delighted her in those last days. But now I am alone and have no one I can trust—my nephew is a wastrel. It would be folly to entrust it to him. Agatha and I discussed it. He would simply sell it away to the highest bidder with no thought to scholarship or what light it can shed on our already accumulated knowledge of ancient texts. Therefore, I leave it in the hands of Providence. I have carefully constructed a method for it to be found. Nothing too simple that it can be worked out straightaway, but challenging enough that it will be a task to reach the end. If you are reading this missive, then you are the new possessor of this precious gift. Handle it carefully. The responsibility rests with you.'"

Poppy looked up, her eyes wide. "Blimey."

"Well said, Sis." Robert seemed more subdued than he had been earlier. "Ivan, you better figure out who we should have look at this."

---

Zoe and Jack stepped out of the hotel elevator into the lobby the next evening. "Poppy didn't say why she wanted us to come to Staircase House?" Jack asked.

"No, she only said she had news that she wanted to share with us in person. I hope she's still a satisfied client," Zoe said as they crossed the lobby. When Zoe and Jack left Staircase House last night, Poppy had certainly been happy, glowingly happy even, but Zoe was sure that had more to do with the budding relationship between Poppy and Ivan than the successful recovery of the painting (for the second time) and the discovery of the ancient book. Zoe and Jack had spent the day answering questions for the police. By the time they'd finished, the sun had set, and they'd returned to the hotel to pack and prep for their flight, which Jack had rescheduled for the next day.

Jack held open the heavy glass door to the street, but Zoe turned back when she heard her name called. A desk clerk hurried across the tile floor, carrying a small square vase filled with a mix of gerbera daisies, mums, and pale cream roses. "This just arrived for you, Mrs. Andrews." The woman handed them to Zoe and shot a conspiratorial grin at Jack before returning to the front desk.

"Oh, Jack, these are gorgeous, but you didn't have to."

"I hate to admit it, but I didn't."

"What?"

"I didn't send those. At this moment, I wish I had, but I didn't. Do I need to be worried? Got another admirer?"

Zoe tilted her head. "I think we're past that stage, don't you? You're the only one for me. So this must be a mistake." Zoe caught sight of a card with her name on it.

She pulled the envelope out and handed the flowers to Jack so she could open it. She read it aloud, "'Congratulations on the successful conclusion of your first assignment. Well done. Harrington.'" Zoe took the flowers back and inhaled. "That was so nice of him."

Jack said, "Hmm, with Harrington around, I can see that

I'm going to have to step up my game. Not many employers send their consultants flowers. Of course, not many consultants have their first job turn out to be so convoluted either."

"I guess this means that Poppy is still happy. I doubt Harrington would have sent these if she'd complained to him."

"What does she have to complain about?" Jack asked.

"I don't know, but I suspect she's one of those people who usually finds something wrong."

"Then let's go see her. I bet you're completely mistaken."

"I hope so," Zoe said as they returned to the elevator to drop the flowers off in their hotel room.

When they arrived at Staircase House, Ivan opened the door and invited them in. Poppy was all smiles and offered them coffee or a drink, which Zoe and Jack declined. "Then come in and sit down. I thought you'd want to know what's happened. All of this is supposed to be hush-hush, but it seems there are leaks already." She frowned up at the minstrel's gallery. Looking up, Zoe caught a glimpse of Robert as he paced to the railing then turned away, his cell phone pressed to his ear.

Ivan, who had taken a seat beside Poppy, put his arm along the back of the sofa behind her. "He can't help it if he's getting calls."

"Yes, but I suspect he made a few of his own," Poppy said then shook her head and leaned back against Ivan's side. "Anyway, I thought you deserved an update since you were instrumental in finding the Foley Codex."

"Foley Codex?" Zoe asked. "Does that mean..."

"It sounds fancy but it's just a name for the book," Ivan

said. "It's what they're calling it while they do the tests and examine it."

"Ivan was right," Poppy said. "It is extremely old, from the first century and—well, you should tell them Ivan."

"The underwriting is an early copy of the Gospel of Mark, which was the earliest Gospel recorded. Tests are still preliminary, but it looks as if it is complete. If it dates to before the fourth century," Ivan raised his hand, "well, it will be a phenomenon. It could be the earliest complete gospel ever discovered."

"And extremely valuable," Jack said.

"Yes," Poppy said, "but we—Robert, Ivan, and I—have agreed to donate it to the university. We're having the legal paperwork arranged."

Zoe blinked. "That's very generous of you." And it wasn't at all what Zoe had expected to be the outcome of their little treasure hunt.

Poppy said, "Well, it took quite a bit of talking to convince Robert that it was the way to go, but it was what the sisters wanted. There was something about Annabel's letter...she went to such trouble to insure it was safe, and then saying she left it to Providence..." Poppy shifted. "After reading that, we all realized the codex wasn't just a means to wealth. Annabel went to such lengths to protect it, creating the riddle, putting the code on the back of the other painting and sending it to her cousin in Salzburg, then creating the storage spot for the book here in Edinburgh, where her nephew rarely visited. I did some digging into Agatha's letters. She mentioned how much he detested Staircase House. He preferred London so I imagine they were fairly certain he wouldn't visit here and find the painting by some fluke. And then she set up the trust for the house to insure it couldn't be sold or remodeled, all the while trusting that the person or people who found it would do the right thing. It was...well, the only way to put it is that it was entrusted to us, and we had a responsibility to make sure it was handled properly. Some of us saw it that way sooner than others..." her voice trailed off as she looked overhead. "But it is all settled now. This way, it can be studied and examined, but we've stipulated that it must also be on display, too. The sisters didn't want it hidden away so that only scholars could see it. They wanted it available to everyone."

Ivan leaned forward and said in a lower voice, "The fact that we agreed to let Robert handle the media attention and the rights for any print or movie deals, helped convince him."

"Really? You think there will be a book deal?" Zoe asked.

"Yes, the media has already picked up the story. He's had three calls about it today, and an option for the movie rights has already come up," Ivan said.

"That sounds perfect for Robert," Zoe said, and she could picture him savoring the media attention, charming television hosts as he relayed the story.

Poppy said, "He'll probably have a ghostwriter lined up by tomorrow, which is fine because I don't want to deal with any of that media stuff." She shuddered. "No, I'd much rather focus on the museum." Poppy scooted forward a bit and said, "I'm going to turn this place into a museum, devoted to the Foley sisters. Once Mother heard the whole story of what had happened with the Foley Codex, she agreed that we shouldn't try to sell Staircase House. We'll catalogue, collect, and display Annabel's paintings, and we'll have Agatha's books and notes here for historians to consult." Poppy looked toward Ivan. "Ivan is going to help me with the antiquarian books."

"Sounds perfect," Zoe said.

"We'll host school field trips and have art lessons for kids and maybe adults." She turned suddenly to Ivan. "What about talks? We should host talks about Victorian travel, art, and books. The talks could be interactive, too. We could have a display recreating Agatha and Annabel's travel kit or maybe a stuffed camel. Agatha wrote about riding a camel. Kids would love something like that."

Ivan laughed. "Sounds excellent. I'll leave it to you to find a camel."

"It shouldn't be too hard..."

Zoe and Jack listened to their plans a little longer then admired *A View of Edinburgh,* which was again hanging on the wall, before they left. As they crossed the close, Zoe said, "I think they just wanted someone to share their plans with."

"I think that was part of it."

"I can't believe they're giving up the treasure, though. Do you think they'll do it, donate it?"

Jack put his hands in his pockets and stared in front of him. "I think so. Robert is playing it like a true businessman. He recognizes that he'll get a lot of value from the story itself, and donating it so that the public has access to it will only build goodwill toward him and his family. I'm sure he'll be front and center, riding the wave of public interest as long as he can."

"A real-life Indiana Jones," Zoe murmured as they walked along. "I can see it. He'll probably take to wearing a fedora."

"Let's hope he skips the whip."

"I'm surprised that Ivan agreed to donate it as well," Zoe said. "At the airport he seemed pretty intent on getting his cut. He even had a contract drawn up."

"But he's in love, so his brain is good and addled. You can look daggers at me all you want. But you know it's true. You saw the way they were looking at each other. He'd probably go along with whatever Poppy suggested right now."

"I guess it will be quite a coup for him, too. Not many librarians recover centuries old books worth millions," Zoe said.

"I'm sure his library will have a new appreciation for him. If he's smart, he'll do what Robert is, and parlay that into a promotion or something."

They turned the corner, and the hotel came into sight. "So, back home for us tomorrow," Zoe said with a sigh. "Good-bye treasure hunting, hello bills and receipts. I'm dreading putting together an expense report for Harrington's assistant," Zoe said, thinking of all the crumpled bits of paper floating about her pockets and messenger bag.

"Maybe we can put that off for a day or two," Jack said as he pulled a box from his pocket. "I got you something, too, to celebrate closing your first case. It's not flowers, but I think you'll like it. You told me girls like this kind of thing."

Zoe took the flat box from him. It was small enough that at first she thought it was jewelry, but the box was too heavy. She pried off the lid and found a padlock nestled in a bed of tissue.

"A lock?" It took her a second to work it out then she smiled widely. "Oh, Jack. Can we?"

"Go back to Salzburg? I think we have to." He turned the lock over. He'd written their names on it in permanent marker. "So what do you say? Can those receipts wait a day or two?"

She put her arms around his neck. "Definitely."

---

Get exclusive excerpts of upcoming books and member-only giveaways at SaraRosett.com/signup.

## THE STORY BEHIND THE STORY

Thanks for reading *Devious*. I hope you enjoyed revisiting Zoe and Jack as much as I did. If you'd like an update when I have a new book out, you can sign up for my updates at SaraRosett.com/signup. It's the best way to stay up-to-date on books from me.

If you enjoyed *Devious*, I'd appreciate it if you posted an online review. Even something as short as a few lines can help potential readers figure out whether or not the book is their cup of tea. Thanks!

Agatha and Annabel Foley are fictitious, but my research about Victorian lady travelers inspired the characters, especially Agnes Smith Lewis and her sister Margaret Dunlop Gibson, world-traveling twin sisters who discovered an important codex in a remote monastery in Sinai. I very much enjoyed Janet Soskice's account of their adventures in her book, *The Sisters of Sinai: How Two Lady Adventurers Discovered the Hidden Gospels*. You can read Agnes' first-hand description of their journey to Egypt, Sinai, and the Holy Land in *Eastern Pilgrims: The Travels of Three Ladies* by Agnes Smith Lewis. The preparations described in Agatha's journals in *Devious* are based on Agnes's description of how she and her traveling companions prepared for their journey. Another adventurous Victorian female was Marianne North, who circled the globe, often traveling alone. She completed over 800 paintings of plants in their native environments. All of these women inspired me, contributing to the creation of Agatha and Annabel Foley.

The million-pound codex that Ivan refers to in the story does exist. It is the Codex Zacynthius, and it contains an undertext. Cambridge University Library raised one million pounds in September 2014 to purchase the codex from the British and Foreign Bible Society, according to the Daily Mail.com.

Staircase House is based on Lady's Stair House in Edinburgh, which is now a museum dedicated to three famous Scottish writers, Robert Burns, Sir Walter Scott, and Robert Louis Stevenson. I visited it on my research trip to Edinburgh. Both Edinburgh and Salzburg are wonderful cities, and I thoroughly enjoyed my research trips to each one. Check out the *Devious pinboard* to see places in Edinburgh and Salzburg that inspired me while I was writing *Devious*.

# ABOUT THE AUTHOR

*USA Today* bestselling author Sara Rosett writes fun mysteries. Her books are light-hearted escapes for readers who enjoy interesting settings, quirky characters, and puzzling mysteries. Publishers Weekly called Sara's books, "satisfying," "well-executed," and "sparkling."

Sara loves to get new stamps in her passport and considers dark chocolate a daily requirement. Find out more at Sara-Rosett.com.

*Connect with Sara*
www.SaraRosett.com

# OTHER BOOKS BY SARA ROSETT

This is Sara's complete catalogue at the time of publication, but new books are in the works. To be the first to find out when Sara has a new book, sign up for her updates at SaraRosett.com/signup.

## *On the Run* series

*Elusive*

*Secretive*

*Deceptive*

*Suspicious*

*Devious*

*Treacherous*

## *Murder on Location* series

*Death in the English Countryside*

*Death in an English Cottage*

*Death in a Stately Home*

*Death in an Elegant City*

*Menace at the Christmas Market (novella)*

*Death in an English Garden*

*Death at an English Wedding*

Made in the USA
Middletown, DE
26 February 2019